MOON CONTRACT

Bringing REAL into PNR

LORE NICOLE

Contents

Dedication

T his book is for all the people out there who have felt less than because of chronic pain and other events not within their control. Never think that you have to hide it all, or that reaching out and advocating for yourself is an overreaction. YOU DESERVE happiness. YOU DESERVE all options possible for having a better quality of living. YOU DESERVE LIFE.

Chapter 1

Looking in the mirror, Lilian placed her hand on her stomach. It wasn't as noticeable from the front, but then she turned to the side and let out a huge sigh. Why did she torture herself by keeping a mirror? Lilian didn't really know. Thankfully, it was fall now with cool mornings, and she could throw on a sweatshirt.

After picking out a random black hoodie, she brushed her blonde hair into a ponytail and went to the kitchen. Met by the usual silence, she grabbed some pain relievers to swallow with water and her breakfast banana before heading out the door to walk to school. While Lilian loved being outside, the mile-long walk to school was tough when she was in constant pain. It wasn't like she could afford a car when she couldn't hold a job due to the chronic pain either.

Often on these walks, she would wish she had parents like the other kids her age. But then she would wonder if it would have even changed anything. Lilian's mom had died during childbirth. Her birth. Her dad couldn't even look at Lilian without feeling disgusted. Blaming her for killing his mate. The Luna, the Alpha's wife, had to help care for Lilian; otherwise, she would have died from starvation and neglect. Her dad still couldn't handle coping with his life and decided to end it with pills. Lilian often blamed him for taking the easy way out and abandoning her, but then she would also speculate whether he died painlessly—as she often contemplated trying to end this life of physical pain she had to endure as a female.

Walking through the academy doors, Lilian waded through the sea of teens. She tried to make herself seem small to avoid drawing attention to herself. All the kids were talking about their upcoming weekend plans, laughing, and carefree, while Lilian suffered and preferred not to attempt smiling and nodding like she fit in with any of them. She did pick up on a couple keywords. Reminders of more suffering to come. Full

Moon. Wolf party. Mystic Woods. Of course, she was in all this pain with the full moon coming. Rejecting her ability to shift was already painful, and now she had to add in her bloat, cramps, stomach problems, and back pain. Just great.

Feeling even less optimistic about the day, she arrived at the empty classroom to take a seat in the back. She walked down the neat row of metal school desks while the scent of old chalk from the board filled her nose. No matter how clean the teachers tried to get the boards the smell would stay forever. These desks had the tops attached to the chairs with a basket hanging under the seat. These only worked well for right-handed students. Thankfully, she was a righty but she didn't like to see some of the students suffer trying to use them.

Dropping her backpack underneath the desk, she slouched into her seat and started taking out the things she would need for her first class. The other students would start coming soon, but they had to go to their lockers and finish their conversations before the bell rang. Lilian considered her bag to be her locker. It not only saved time between classes to just have everything with her, but it also saved on walking. Just a few extra steps to go to her actual locker to exchange books were torture these days.

Just as she had placed her head on top of her book to rest a moment, the first bell rang. It echoed in her head and caused her to flinch as she noticed her headache was still there. It also warned her to brace herself just before the mob of teens hurried for their classrooms, including the one she was in. Along with them came the teacher with her briefcase and coffee in hand. She was newer to the school, younger as well. Most of these teachers were graying and less than sympathetic, their empathy worn down over time. Professor Jones looked fresh with her shiny light brown hair and glittering green eyes. Lilian watched Professor Jones as she settled her things on her desk and did her scan of the students. Lilian felt when the eyes landed on her and looked up to see sympathy in the teacher's eyes.

Apparently, the teachers all knew when Lilian wore a sweatshirt that she wouldn't be able to focus well in class. She only wore one on days she was in pain or bloated. Most teachers would leave her alone, asking questions of other students. However, in her third class, Professor Lawson would purposely call her out in hopes she messed up. He seemed to enjoy her being laughed at and teased by her classmates. *Asshole*. But over these last years of high school, Lilian had gotten smart and would read ahead for his class. Be one step ahead of him.

This caused many classmates to get bored with him trying to torture her. Except for Chad. He was the Alpha's second son. He was also good-looking and popular; fitting the typical blonde haired, blue-eyed quarterback of the football team stereotype. You would think he would have all the attention he would ever need or want, but Chad seemed to relish tormenting her, whether or not he got reactions from the crowd. He also just happened to be in almost every class with her, including this one. Just hearing his snide voice from across the room caused her to grimace. Some girls seemed to love his deep voice, but when he teased it became higher pitched and grated on her nerves.

She spent most of the class trying to focus on what the teacher was saying while trying not to fall asleep or throw up. It was really a toss-up which would happen first if she didn't keep her willpower strong. It wasn't that Lilian found statistics boring, or nauseating, but the constant sharp, stabbing pains took their toll. She was glad when the bell finally rang, signaling the swarm to move on to their next destinations. Slowly, Lilian stood up and lifted her bag at the same time, so she didn't have to bend over for it. Letting out a sigh, she followed the last of the kids out the door, just to turn into another classroom two doors down. One class finished, seven more to go. Plus, lunch in the clique-filled cafeteria. Resigned to the rest of the day already, she once again found a seat in the back and settled in. Rinse and Repeat...

So close to getting through another class, something started to feel different. Warmth built inside Lilian's chest. It felt good, but she didn't know what it was from. She had never felt it before. But it was soon followed by another feeling she recognized, and she tensed up, preparing for more pain. Lilian tried to keep her wolf contained and controlled, quiet. However, this heat caused her wolf to perk up and stretch in her mind's eye. While she could see the action in her mind, she could also feel them. The stretching was in her abdomen, and with that area already in pain, the extension caused her to hug her stomach tight, and a moan slipped out.

These actions caught the teacher's and students' attention, who all decided to quiet down and stare.

Professor Miller wrinkled her brow in worry and then gave a little smile as she offered Lilian an escape. "Lilian, would you like to go to the nurse's office?" Not wanting to stay and be stared at, Lilian nodded with tears in her eyes. She stood up to put her things into her bag, hoping to leave as fast as possible. Then she heard it. Chad's voice.

"Ooo, is Lilian PREGNANT?" he teased loudly. Of course, he would notice her bulging belly, even with the sweatshirt on. He would never miss something he could use as a weapon against her. A few classmates snickered, giving him encouragement for more. "Who would even sleep with you?" he tormented. "You're just a STRAY dog." The tears coming down her face were no longer from pain, but from the shame he made her feel.

She could feel her wolf trying to growl inside of her. Trying to defend her even though her classmates couldn't see her. Lilian refused to let the growl come out of her own lips. She couldn't give the Alpha's son any reaction that could be seen as aggression. As the Alpha's son, he was protected; even the teachers couldn't do anything against him. All they could do was let the Alpha and Luna know about any incidents and let them choose to handle it or just shrug it off. If Lilian reacted, she could be punished by the bully himself, or the teachers, just for the indiscretion.

Chapter 2

Trying to ignore Chad, Lilian gathered her books into her bag. While gritting her teeth, she noticed the warmth was getting hotter, and her ears picked up on footsteps coming towards their classroom door. Listening to the steps and the knob turning helped her ignore whatever Chad was trying to throw her way. No one else had noticed the visitor behind the door who paused opening it, as though listening to Chad's antics.

Apparently, after having heard enough, the door flew open. Its handle bounced off the wall with a loud crash, revealing the person behind it holding a large duffle bag. All eyes were on the visitor, including Chad's, as he made an audible gulp. The stranger, who looked like an older version of Chad, yelled, "What the HELL are you doing, Chad?! You were raised better than to bully others, especially a female of our own pack."

Trying to backpedal and make excuses, Chad replied, "Dylan, she's just the stray living in the extra pack house."

"And you think that makes it fine to tease? Anyone can lose their parents at any time, including us, and teasing someone, who is obviously in pain, about their living status is even worse. As an Alpha's son, you should respect ALL pack members to earn their respect. You never know when you might need someone's help or who their mate will turn out to be."

While this Dylan guy continued to make Chad feel small, Lilian took her chance to scurry out of the room towards the nurse's office. She could still hear Dylan's voice behind her since she left the door wide open. She paused to listen to what else he was saying.

"Mom had me bring your football gear YOU left at home to you for practice. You would have thought being the team captain meant you know what it takes to be a leader. I'm guessing they gave you the title because of who you are and not because you actually earned it." Letting the sting of his words hit, he dropped the duffle at the door and left, heading towards where Lilian stood.

Lilian watched as this gorgeous guy walked toward her. No one really ever "saw" her, so for this dark-haired, blue-eyed college student to come up to her rendered her speechless.

"Are you okay?" he asked Lilian softly, placing a finger under her chin so she would look at him instead of her shoes. That slight touch sent a shiver down her spine that curled low in her belly where the warmth had gathered. She had never felt that before but had a good idea what it could be, especially as her wolf rumbled a soft purr. Destiny wanted them together, as fated mates.

Dylan kept his gaze on her as her eyes widened, and she backed away. She whispered, "You can't want me. I'm broken." Then she dashed away from him as fast as she could. Not caring about her physical pain, Lilian ran past the nurse's office and left right out through the school's front doors. The backpack bounced on her sore back, and after a mile, she had to stop to sit down alongside the dirt road that led to her home. She ruffled through her bag to find her bottle of water and extra pain pill supply. After taking a few, she sat and tried to stretch her muscles until her cramps stabbed her like her ovaries were battling it out with tiny, sharp shivs.

Lilian thought back on what happened at school. Of course it would be the future Alpha her wolf would be fated to mate. How could fate be so cruel as to punish him with her? The whole deal with fated mates was that they were supposed to balance each other out, mate to solidify their union, and helped to birth the next generation, especially the alphas.

Tears returned to Lilian's eyes as she remembered telling Dylan she was broken. The sobs started when she realized they could never be together. It was bad enough that when she turned eighteen in September, she couldn't sense her mate in school. She thought that maybe her health issues just made her "unmate-able". But knowing that her fated mate was older, which was why he wasn't there, at least took that self-deprecating notion away. It was still a curse because she knew she would never be accepted as a Luna, even if Dylan wanted her. If he ever found out.

Still sitting on the grassy roadside, indulging in self-pity, the sound of a rumbling truck got louder as it neared. Assuming it was just another pack member heading to a pack house, she didn't bother looking up. Maybe if she kept her head down, they wouldn't pay her any notice and just keep going. Save her the embarrassment of showing her tear-soaked cheeks.

To her horror, Lilian heard the gravel crunch and shift as the truck applied breaks, dust wafting up and towards her from the wind. Trying to not move, still curled in a ball to look small and blend in, Lilian could feel her body begin to shake. The truck shifted into park, and the door creaked open. She listened as the gravel ground under footsteps, getting louder as the person came closer. *Why, of all days, do I finally get noticed today?*

The hand on her shoulder was something like an electrical shock, and the warmth from earlier returned. *Oh no. Of course, it's him and seeing me at my low. Shit.*

"Are you okay?" he asked, his voice a low whisper as if he was afraid she would be scared and run like a frightened mouse again. Not wanting to let him hear her cry, she kept her head down and just shook it in reply. "I didn't think so," she heard before his arms encircled her. One arm swooped under her legs as his other wrapped around her back. He lifted her and her bag with ease, and she leaned against his chest in resignation. "If you can grab the handle to open the door, I'll set you on the seat and give you a ride the rest of the way home."

Still refusing to show face, she peeked enough to spot the handle and did as he asked. It took him a moment to set her down, and she wondered if he felt the same warmth and connection she did. Once he let her go to walk around to his own side, the warmth started to fade, and she found she missed it. Before he climbed in, Lilian sighed with the loss, still believing in her brokenness and knowing she would have to break their bond by refusing him. She heard that bond-breaking is painful, but in the long run, she thought it would be the best for his sake as the future Alpha. Plus, it wasn't like Lilian was a stranger to pain. She lived with it every day.

The drive was only a couple minutes, which probably would have taken her almost half an hour unless the ibuprofen had started to work, and it was spent in silence. Lilian hoped the tear stains and redness would have faded by now. She knew she would have to face Dylan, and she wanted at least a small bit of dignity. The truck stopped in the driveway to her place, just a small white cottage that was plenty big enough for just her.

"Would you like me to carry you again, or do you think you can walk?"

Wanting to not seem weak, she grabbed the door's handle and pushed it open. Gripping her bag tight, she climbed out. Her feet hit the ground, and her knees buckled with the stabbing pelvic pain. She stumbled but managed to hold onto the door to steady herself. She felt a strong arm wrap around her for support and realized that she had never even heard Dylan get out of the truck. She felt his other arm go around front to take the bag from her hands.

"Let's try to walk. I'm here for you," he said softly with sincerity. She nodded, gritting her teeth to stop from letting out any pain-filled groans. She took one slow step and then another. It was slow going, but he let her be her stubborn self and stayed with her the entire time. She was shocked. Most of her life was filled with neglect or bullies. She had no idea how to react to this gentle and caring act. She wanted to push him away, yet also to hold him close. Tell him to leave but wrap her arms around him. Why did she have to be broken? Not only was she in physical torture but mental turmoil now too.

When they reached the house, Dylan helped her up the front steps and opened the door for her. Lilian never locked her door. Besides being a pack house, she didn't have anything worth stealing. On days when she needed to get inside quickly and curl up on her bed or couch in pain, that lock was just a hindrance. Dylan let her go in, thinking she could make it to the living room couch just arm's length away. The couch was dark blue and showed signs of wear in its faded spots, small tears, and there wasn't much left of its cushioning. He closed the door behind him and set her bag down, then went to her kitchen to find her something to eat, pain meds, and anything else that might help. Instead, he found a bare fridge and mostly bare cupboards; no food, just basic dishes left unused.

"Do you have any other pain pills or food? You shouldn't take anything on an empty stomach, and I know you left before lunch."

Tears beaded in Lilian's eyes. "I had a banana for breakfast and have Tylenol in my bookbag."

"That's it?" he asked, astonished. Lilian couldn't even look at him as she gave him a little nod. "That's not going to help you much."

"What do you expect?" she started. "I have no parents and can never hold a job for long with this pain. Trust me when I say I've often thought I'd be better off following in my father's footsteps."

Dylan's stare became steely as his anger rose. "Don't you get any food or aid from the pack?"

"I got this house to use, but once I became more self-sufficient, your mom stopped coming to check on me."

"My mom never told you about pack resources?"

All Lilian could do was shake her head. She didn't want to see him angry, but she also didn't want to risk angering him more by not answering.

"Don't worry. I'm not angry at you, Lilian. If you were never told, then you wouldn't know about them. Someone should have informed you. That's why I'm angry. The pack has failed YOU. You haven't failed us." Hearing his words, she couldn't stop the tears from streaming down her face any longer or the sobs she had tried holding back. He pulled a cell phone from his pants pocket. She could see him giving orders angrily but quiet enough that she couldn't hear.

He soon finished his call and sat beside her on the couch. She tried to move over for him, but the cramps wouldn't let her. Instead, he gently took the small space next to her and shifted her so that she lay in his lap. He still held his phone and used it to play a few comedy videos hoping to take away her tears. He took the hair tie out and stroked her hair with his free hand, a move that made her think this was what her mother would do had she still been alive to care for her. It was so tender and sweet, slowly melting away Lilian's barriers to keep him away for his own sake...

Chapter 3

L ilian was finally calm and found herself dozing off as Dylan kept brushing her hair with his fingers while they laughed at the videos. She nearly landed on the floor when a knock on her door caused her to jump in surprise. Clutching her stomach, she couldn't stop the word "crap" from leaving her lips. "Sorry," Dylan apologized. "I should have warned you that I was having someone stop in."

He helped her sit up on the couch as he stood up and answered the door. Opening the door wide, Dylan let another guy around his age into her house with his arms full of bags. Lilian thought she might have seen him before, but it was hard to say since she didn't go out on social visits. "Thank you, Dan," Dylan said to him. "Go ahead and set them in the kitchen on the counter."

With his arms emptied, Dan turned back to look back at Dylan and saw Lilian on the couch. "Would you like me to put anything away?" he offered.

"Nah. I'll take care of it," Dylan responded. "By the way, Dan, meet Lilian. My mate. Lilian, this is Daniel, my Beta in command, or will be when we take over," he clarified.

Oh, no. He called me his MATE. In front of Daniel, his beta! We never even talked about it. Heck, I wasn't going to admit to it. I was going to let him get out of being my mate since I didn't want him stuck with me. Broken and with no value. Can he rescind his introduction of me with Daniel? Oh, no. Thoughts were racing through her mind and she couldn't even find the words to have him take his own back. Heck, she could barely manage a "thank you, Daniel," before the second nicest guy she's ever known took his leave out her door.

When her door closed behind Daniel, she couldn't help but ask Dylan for clarification. "Did you, did you just introduce me as your mate to your beta?"

"Well, yeah," he replied, shrugging his shoulders, as he removed items from their bags to see what Daniel had brought for them. "You can't tell me that you don't feel the mate bond?" he asked her with confusion tinting his voice.

"Of course I do. But I already told you I'm broken. I'm worthless for anyone as a mate." While she wanted to cry with that admission, she took a deep breath to find what small amount of strength she had. She didn't want to be mateless for the rest of her life, but she also didn't want anyone to feel stuck. Lilian decided better now than never to have this conversation with Dylan. At least they hadn't officially announced their bond to his family or solidified the bond during mating heat.

"You might feel broken down from living in pain and with lack of any support these last few years, but you are nowhere close to worthless," he sternly told her.

"Mates are supposed to be able to mate and raise the next generation, especially for Alphas and Lunas. The pain that I am having has to do with that future. It may be a future that I cannot have. I can't be a Luna if I cannot have children," she finished. Her voice became firmer with every word as she tried to make him see that they shouldn't even try being together.

"Have you been to a doctor for it yet?"

"No."

"Then how do you know for certain that you can't have kids or that there isn't a cure?"

She had to admit that she didn't know those things. "It's a feeling I have."

"So you are going to give up a future of us being together as mates on just a feeling?"

"Well, it's not like I can go to a doctor," she retorted.

"And why can't you?"

"I have no parents for medical insurance and no money coming in right now to pay for anything myself. A doctor's visit and any test they want to run are not within my budget. Trust me, there were several times I wanted to go to the ER but held off and just tried to survive."

Several emotions flashed across Dylan's face. It was like he didn't know if he wanted to be angry, to cry, or if he was...proud? Lilian watched as he sat the last bag aside and walked over to kneel in front of her. He grabbed her hands and held them in her lap.

"Lilian. You have been so strong, trying to live on your own while in such pain. I can't even imagine. My heart breaks hearing you talk about pain that makes you wish for the ER or death. I wish my mother, or someone from our pack, would have given you the information for all the resources we have. It could have helped you so much by now, especially knowing the pack has full coverage insurance for every pack member, even you. There's also a pack grocery and clothing center near my parents' home which, even I, as future Alpha, have been to." He paused to collect his growing anger and calm himself.

When ready, he continued, "This is what I mean by the pack having failed you, and I am so sorry. If I had known, I would have stepped in sooner. As it is, I am here now and can only hope to make up for our pack's mistakes."

Lilian just sat there and took in his words. It was hard to comprehend. She could have been to a doctor and received help all these years. Struggling to hold a job and feed herself, when she could have gotten food from this pack's center.

While she wanted to be angry about not knowing, she couldn't help but say, "It isn't just your mom's, or the pack's, fault. I also never asked your mom for help figuring anything out. I relied on the internet at school for answers. Those were human answers, of course, and not pack. That idiocy is mine. So don't be hard on your mom but let's just go forward fresh from here?" Lilian offered. Then she added, "I still think you would be better off with someone else as a mate."

"Let me decide who is good enough," he told her. "You have been independent, strong, and smart. You also seem to have loyalty to our pack even though you have received nothing but bullying from my brother and your classmates. Those are all qualities I love. The pain you have? I am here for you now and will help you through it. Always." He sounded so sincere and final in his declaration that Lilian couldn't help but agree with him.

Thinking she finally believed him, Dylan released her hands and stood up. He went back to the kitchen to put things away so nothing fresh could spoil. Besides typical grocery staples like milk and bread, Daniel had brought over several containers from various fast food places. Before putting them away, he asked, "Do you feel like spaghetti, pizza, chicken noodle soup, or orange chicken and lo mein?"

Lilian had never had that many choices before. She figured she had eaten frozen pizza and canned spaghetti and soups before. "Um, how about the orange chicken and whatever you said was with it?"

"Lo mein?"

"Yeah, that," she said.

Dylan put the rest of the food away and then split the Chinese containers in half on the paper plates in the bag with them. He grabbed a couple forks from a kitchen drawer and then served her before sitting down himself. She wondered if eating with her was his way of making sure she ate. She stabbed a small piece of orange sauce-covered meat with her fork and tried a bite. It was sweet yet sour. She also tried a bite of the dark noodles, with a sauce she didn't know the name for, with bits of vegetable slivers running through them. She moaned at the taste, eyes closed, as she savored the food.

"You have never had Chinese food before, have you?" Dylan asked. He looked entertained by her reactions.

Lilian could feel the blush staining her cheeks. He probably ate these foods all the time. Her lack of food experience was embarrassing to her. She ducked her head while trying to eat more. Feeling self-conscious wouldn't stop her from eating the rest to show him that she did, in fact, eat, and he could go home if he wanted. *If.* It wasn't like she could tell the future

Alpha to get out of his own pack house. But the idea of trying made her smile a little.

"Is that a smile I see?" he teased.

"Yes. I was just thinking how funny it would be of me if I tried to get you to leave when this is a pack house, and you are the future Alpha."

"Do you want me to leave?" he asked. "I will if you want me to. I don't want to but will respect your wishes."

How could fate have given her such a great, understanding guy and yet a broken mate in her? "No. It is kinda nice not being so alone for once," she admitted.

"Haven't you had friends over?"

"What friends? No friends want to hang out with someone that can't socialize because they are always in pain. No one wants to hear complaining all the time. Heck, I don't even want to be friends with myself. How can I fault anyone else for not sticking around?"

"Well, you have me now. I will stick to you like burrs in fur," Dylan joked, but his voice still held a note of seriousness. Not thinking or wanting to think, Lilian decided just to trust things for once and leaned into him for comfort. He stayed in place and continued eating so she wouldn't get nervous and move away, like a caretaker would with an abandoned dog in a shelter trying to earn their trust.

She continued eating as well. She was trying to relax and put her trust in fate, hoping it knew what it was doing with their lives. Dylan let off a warmth that helped soothe her and put even her wolf at peace. Her pain seemed to have dimmed as well. The full moon was coming, and she wasn't crippled in pain for once. With a mate by her side, she could almost imagine what being normal was like. While he couldn't yet change her mind about being broken, at least she could begin to feel hope. Especially now that she knew she could actually go to a doctor and receive treatment. That, itself, was a life changer for Lilian.

Chapter 4

Several hours had passed since they had eaten Chinese together. They spent the time together as if they were never interrupted by Daniel's delivery. Lilian lay on the couch, her head resting on Dylan's lap, as they continued watching different movies and tv shows on his phone until it was almost out of power. She enjoyed the calming time together and learning about Dylan. Lilian could tell what jokes he enjoyed, what shows he liked to watch the most, and that he had no issue speaking his mind if a movie got something wrong. When his phone was close to dying, she almost wanted to hate it, as if the phone was impeding their time together.

"I have a charger in my truck," he told her. "Why don't you warm up the pizza for us while I go and get it?"

Lilian felt pretty good since eating lunch earlier and keeping up on pain pills. Maybe part of it was just having her mate beside her. Could the bond influence pain? If so, she never wanted him to leave. She sat up on the couch to let him stand up, then stood herself. "How many slices do you want?"

"Just a couple will be enough for me. Make sure to get yourself enough to help coat your stomach if you need more pain relievers." Lilian couldn't help but smile at his concern for her. It was new for her to get used to, but she liked the feeling it gave her. Lilian didn't want to let him down or make him wait. As he went to his truck, she hurried into the kitchen to get plates of pizza and warmed them in the microwave. They were ready before he came back in. Getting his charger shouldn't have taken that long, and she was starting to get curious. She sat the plates on the coffee table and went to open the door to take a peek.

"Just in time," Dylan smiled at her from the other side of her doorway. "It's a full moon tonight, and I didn't want to leave you alone." He held up a duffle bag and carried it inside past her. "As the future Alpha, I'm often called on surprise road trips, so I keep a bag packed and ready."

Where will he sleep? she wondered. While she sometimes slept on the couch, it was old, and the coils could be felt in the cushions the longer they were laid on. She had never even had a friend over, let alone a boy or her mate, before. She turned red. "I only have one bed, but it is big enough if you want to share it." It wasn't really that wrong to offer if he was her mate, was it?

He must have noticed her blushing as he replied, "Don't worry. I have pajama pants in my bag."

He probably has experience. Way more than I do. How many beds has he slept in with other girls? She wasn't going to ask. Not only would it not be polite, but she probably didn't want to know. He could probably guess she didn't have any experience in the whole relationship thing since she had a hard time even asking him to share her bed.

Chapter 5

The rest of the evening passed, and Lilian could tell the moon was starting to make its way into their sky. She didn't know if it was just her or if everyone felt the need to shift as much as she did. Her pelvic pain seemed to make her nerves more sensitive. The higher the moon, the more the pain pills would wear off. It was like that every month.

It was barely nine, and already she felt herself starting to shake. She tried to sit up and move away from Dylan before he could notice, but she was too slow. "Are you cold?" he asked. "I will find you a blanket, or you can put on my sweatshirt over yours if you'd like?"

"No, I'm not cold," she told him, gritting her teeth so they wouldn't chatter from the pain. "I can feel the moon rising, and it makes my wolf want to be free.

Wants me to shift. My pain worsens from stretching inside and holding it back."

"You hold back?" he asked, completely shocked. Lilian knew that he just assumed everyone shifted, so she was an abnormality.

"I have never shifted." She hated to admit that, but it was also freeing to finally tell someone. She just hoped he wouldn't think bad about it, about her.

"Never?"

"Nope. I could feel the shifting when I was thirteen, when my pelvic pain started, but I have stopped it every month since."

"But, why not shift?" he asked, trying to make sense of it.

"I have a couple reasons, but they are probably silly," she said, looking down at her hands.

"Well, I'm here and ready to listen."

"I guess I'm just afraid," Lilian started. "I am scared that the shift will hurt me even worse than I already do now. I'm even more afraid that if I shift, I might discover that my wolf shares my pain. If we can't run freely and have the same pain, I don't want to shift and let down my wolf. If she experienced the pain, I would feel so guilty." She finished her confession and waited to hear the criticism. Yet, it never came. She glanced toward Dylan and saw he was deep in thought.

"I am in awe of you," he confessed. "If I were in your position, I probably would have shifted just to try and get any relief possible. You are just completely selfless. You don't blame my mom or the pack for not being there, and you also will do anything to spare your wolf possible pain. I just can't even comprehend how you can go through what you have and stay so loyal and caring." His blue eyes were wide with pride as he shook his head in disbelief. "You are just something else. Something special. No matter what happens, I am proud to be your mate. Proud," he repeated to reinforce his words.

Lilian felt her eyes well up and couldn't help the tears streaming down her face. Sobs wracked her chest and escaped her lips, even though she tried so hard to hold them in. They only got worse when Dylan asked his next questions. "What's the matter? Is the pain worse? Can I get you more ibuprofen?"

Trying hard to pause her crying, she struggled to answer him. "I'm okay. These are happy tears," she choked out.

"Happy tears?" he asked, dumbfounded.

Lilian nodded. "I have never heard anyone say they were proud of me. I've been in this house, by myself, in pain. For years." She paused to try to find more words and hoped they made sense. "You literally walked into my life today and have already been there for me. Helped me so much. Even if you don't choose to be mated to me, I will always appreciate today."

"I already told you I was proud to be your mate. I meant it. You are stuck with me," he said slowly, emphasizing each word, as he took her face into his hands to make her look at him. "YOU are my mate." Even with tears making salty streams down her face and her nose running, he claimed her lips in a kiss. Lilian, of course, had never kissed anyone before and didn't know what to do. She sat there in shock and let Dylan kiss her until he leaned away to look into her eyes. So she could see the truth shining in his eyes. He didn't seem phased by her not returning the kiss. In fact, he seemed pleased with himself.

The moment was broken when pain struck her stomach like a lightning bolt. Lilian leaned into the side of the couch and moaned, trying to get through it, waiting for it to fade away. With Dylan there, she was more concerned over his reaction than she was for herself. He looked like he was feeling helpless and pity for her. "Would you be a little more comfortable in your bed?" he offered.

She barely nodded, and he swooped her off the couch and hurried up the steps to her little room. He helped her stand up and let her go when she seemed stable. "Why don't you try to change into something more comfortable? I'll be right back. I'm just going to grab us a couple of waters and my duffle."

Lilian knew that he would be as quick as he could. Since she was in between the waves of pain, she grabbed her sweatpants and a tank top, taking them to the bathroom. She took her time changing, brushing her teeth, and using the bathroom before she walked back out. Dylan was already sitting on her bed, waiting in his flannel pajama pants. No shirt. She would have admired his athletic form if she wasn't still in pain. *Would shifting and running in wolf form help me tone up too, or does he work out?* she wondered.

She was able to get to her bed on the side opposite of Dylan before the next wave of shooting pain hit. She curled up in a shivering ball, trying not to cry out while waiting for it to pass. As it lessened again, her shivering slowed.

"Okay, for now?" he whispered.

Lilian sat up and nodded. He handed her a bottle of berry-flavored water. She took it with a smile. Her mouth was dry, and she feared her voice wouldn't work. Opening the bottle, she took a big drink from it. She put the cap back on, sat it on her nightstand, and thanked Dylan. "You're welcome," he replied back automatically. "Do you want to try and get some rest?"

"I don't know if I will be able to sleep, but I can try to at least rest in between." She shifted the old, dingy comforter to lay underneath it. Dylan turned off the table lamp beside him, and she felt him trying to get comfortable on top of the blanket in an attempt to give her space.

He had barely stopped moving when she curled up again, wracked with pain. She was shaking even worse than before, yet she could feel Dylan's arms wrap around her. He had joined her under the covers to hold her and comfort her through the pain. She could feel his chest vibrating as his own wolf lightly growled. Her wolf whined in return but settled down. Lilian snuggled back into Dylan's embrace, and they lay there together.

With his wolf having calmed hers down, the pain of stretching from the need to shift faded away. She still could feel her normal pain, but she also felt some relief. Enough that she quickly fell asleep. Whether it was the exhaustion from the battle with pain or the comfort and safety of having her mate enveloping her, she didn't care. She was just grateful for the reprieve. Lilian slept the best she ever had in those long five years of being alone.

Chapter 6

Saturday morning came too quick for Lilian. She woke up still in Dylan's embrace, warm and comfortable. She was too afraid to move in case her pain flared as it often did. She did need a drink and to use the bathroom, though. A sigh escaped her lips, and Dylan tightened his arms, giving her a hug from behind.

"Are you alright?" he asked gently.

"For right now. I just don't want to move, but I have to."

He relaxed his arms and rolled to his back to give her space. If it wasn't for her bladder, Lilian would have rolled over into him and tried to ignore the sunlight streaming through her curtainless, bare windows. She tensed up, preparing herself for discomfort as she slowly pushed herself up. Gingerly standing, she was shocked. While she felt a little sore, it wasn't horrible. If it stayed this way, Lilian would be ecstatic.

She took a quick drink of the water still on her nightstand, then went to the bathroom. She hurried, anxious to return to bed with a nice, warm Dylan. *Um, bed. Yeah. Nice and warm bed.* Except, he wasn't there when she came back out. His bag was still beside the bed, so she knew he didn't leave. Curious, she made her way downstairs.

Halfway down, she heard cupboard doors closing. She peeked around the stairway wall to see what Dylan was up to in the kitchen. On the counter, she spotted bread, eggs, syrup, and ... cinnamon? She was perplexed. The eggs and toast made sense, but not the rest. Pretending she hadn't just watched his butt as he bent over looking for a pan, she walked into the kitchen. "Bathroom is open if you need it." *Oh my gosh. How lame did I just sound?*

"I, uh, went outside already," he responded as he stood up, holding a pan like it was a prize. "Do you have a large bowl?"

Embarrassed at her earlier question, she tried to hide her face with her hair as she walked over to grab a mixing bowl from above the counter near the fridge.

She sat it on the island counter next to his other finds just as he returned with a milk bottle. "What are you making?" she asked, curiosity finally getting the best of her.

"Haven't you ever had French toast?"

Brows furrowed, Lilian shook her head. "I've heard of French fries but not French toast."

This answer seemed to make him happy. Dylan's smile lit up his entire face. "Well, I am very honored that mine will be the first you have ever had. Well, at least how my mom taught me to make it anyway."

Lilian was entertained watching Chef Dylan. She never expected him to know how to cook but, then again, he has been full of surprises since they met yesterday. He looked like a wizard as he mixed sugar, cinnamon, and nutmeg into a small bowl. Then eggs were sacrificed as they were cracked into the larger container. He whisked the eggs, added a quick splash of milk, and then began to sprinkle in the bowl of dry spices. He finished the mix with a bit of vanilla. Setting it off to the side, he warmed up the pan on her stove and melted a little butter.

Lilian was expecting him to just pour the mix in like an omelet but was surprised to see him put a slice of bread into the egg bowl. She watched as he flipped it over so both sides were covered in goo before placing the bread into the pan. He was able to fit four slices in at a time and flipped each in the order they went in. Lilian found herself standing near him just to watch as each side revealed a golden brown color. When he figured the other side looked the same, he flipped them out onto a plate and then did another round to finish using up the egg mix.

Second round complete, Dylan turned off the stove and carried the two plates to the island. He poured enough syrup over each stack to make her teeth hurt, but she was confident he knew what he was doing. She grabbed them each a fork, and they took their plates to the couch.

Lilian wished she had a dining table for them to eat at, but at least with the couch, she could sit beside him. She watched how Dylan cut through the toast and then swiped the layers through the puddle of syrup before taking a bite. Copying him, she was really surprised. The syrup wasn't as sweet with the eggy toast as she expected. The toast wasn't crunchy like plain toast, but it was soft and spongy.

Knowing he was waiting for her reaction, she quickly swallowed her own bite. She knew enough to not talk with her mouth full and made sure it was empty before speaking. "That is amazing! I've never had anything like it before and will have to tell your mom thank you for teaching you."

Lilian could tell that Dylan was proud of himself but held back from preening. He finished eating with a smile that never left his face. When they were done, before she could even stand up, Dylan took her plate to the sink. "You cooked breakfast," she reminded him. "I should be the one to clean up at least."

"You have been cleaning up after yourself and taking care of yourself for five years. I think I can handle doing this for you. Maybe I will let you clean the dishes later." He winked. *Later? Isn't he going to be leaving to go back to his own home? Maybe it was just a slip of the tongue.*

It wasn't like she had television, games to play, or much of anything else. She didn't think Dylan would want to stay here to eat and watch shows on the small cell phone screen. But, he did say later, so maybe he planned to after all.

This whole thing with having a mate, and wondering how a guy thinks, was mind boggling! She didn't remember much about her father, except how absent he was even when they were in the same room. Her only experience was with her classmates; it wasn't like Chad was a shining example. Especially since Dylan seemed to be the complete opposite of his brother. Thankfully.

He cut in through her rambling thoughts. "Why don't you head upstairs and get ready for the day?"

"Get ready?"

"It's going to be a nice day, and you seem to be feeling better, so why spend it inside? I have plans." He smiled at her with excitement over these so-called plans. Lilian was curious about what in the world he could have arranged for them. She hadn't seen him on his phone at all this morning. She concluded there was only one way to find out and went to find something besides pajamas to wear.

Dylan didn't seem to be fancy, and for that, she was thankful. She didn't own any special dresses or shoes. He seemed athletic and casual, which was something she could manage. Lilian spent most of her time wearing loose clothes and had difficulty wearing jeans because of the pain and bloating she had become accustomed to. Her pain was low today, and so was the bloat, by some miracle. To celebrate this small respite and feel a bit sexier, she went with a pair of dark wash jeans and a black tank top with a little beading around the collar line.

She carried the outfit to the bathroom and took a quick shower. She wrapped her hair in a towel to help dry it while doing other tasks like getting dressed and brushing her teeth. Lilian never learned how to do the fancy makeup styles like the others her age, but she put on some eyeshadow, mascara, and lip gloss. Just a little something extra to look like she had made an effort to look nice for Dylan. She didn't know where they would be going and didn't want to be a disappointment to him in front of anyone else.

While Lilian had been getting ready, Dylan must have as well. When she arrived back downstairs, she noticed he was in jeans and a t-shirt. She was slightly disappointed. Not that he didn't look good, but she had become quite fond of him wearing just the flannel pants. The outfit change also proved that he was serious about them going out. She didn't know if she should be excited because she hadn't been out for fun in a long time or anxious. What would happen if the pain came back during their day out? *You know what, Lilian, just go and have fun while it lasts because that is all you can do,* she told herself. She felt her wolf nod in approval at her thoughts. *If my wolf feels fine, then I should too.*

Straightening her shoulders, she left the bottom step. Dylan heard her and turned around from where he waited, leaning on the back of the couch. Lilian saw his eyes widen and felt a little pleased with herself. "Wow," he uttered. "You are beautiful."

Lilian felt herself blush. "Thank you," she softly replied. She cleared her throat and changed the topic away from herself. "Ready to go?"

"I am if you are," he dared her and waved his hand toward the door. Taking his challenge, Lilian took her small purse out of her school bag and walked out to his truck. She was in the passenger seat with the door shut before he had even closed the door behind him. She gave him a smirk and hung onto her handbag as he walked over to his side. Her bag didn't have much money in it, but it did hold the essential over-the-counter pills for just-in-cases. She prayed to

the Moon Goddess that they wouldn't be needed.
Please let me have just this one day.

Chapter 7

The pack houses were considered a suburb of the city Luna Cove, where the main businesses and non-pack members, such as witches, resided. Outside LC were suburbs for the different packs of shifters, from wolves to bears and cats to birds. Since Lilian never traveled outside of the pack area and their own middle school-high school combo, Luna Cove was a treat to see on a Saturday.

There were people *everywhere*. Some were eating at Rosie's Cafe, while others attended a movie playing at the theater. Groups of people stood along the sidewalk, catching up on the week's gossip. There was a small coffee shop, a rustic-looking tavern, and a thrift store each with their usual customers. Lilian wanted to visit every place yet was nervous about visiting any of them. *What if I run into any classmates? Will I bring shame to Dylan and his family?*

Dylan pulled his truck into the movie theater's side parking lot. He turned the key off and hopped out. She was slightly nauseous from all the worrying and hadn't moved yet. "What are you waiting for? Let's go!" Dylan told her with enough excitement for them both. Lilian couldn't help but smile and feel a little excited in return. She got out, slinging her purse over her shoulder, and met Dylan at the back of his truck.

He wrapped his arm around her, placing his hand on her hip and pulling her into him closely. Lilian glanced at him with surprise. He was choosing to claim her as his in public, showing off to anyone who might see them going to the movies that she was his. As they walked to the front, his arm stayed put as they viewed the available movies and air times. Action, romantic comedy, cartoon, even a documentary to choose from.

Giving her a gentle squeeze, Dylan asked, "What do you think? I know we watched comedies yesterday. We could watch another one or go for something different?"

"Let's change it up," she told him. "How about either action or cartoon? I haven't seen any previews, so maybe you should pick one."

"The cartoon one looks pretty decent, and it starts in ten minutes. The other one isn't for an hour." Lilian nodded at his spoken thoughts. "We can always see the other one on a different day, right?"

"Right," she agreed. She had to start reminding herself that her mate actually wanted to stay with her. It was a permanent relationship. They would have time for all sorts of things together. *Will I ever get passed this doubt and stop being surprised at thoughts of another day? Then again, do I ever want to stop being surprised?*

While she had been in her head again, Dylan had guided her through the ticket station, and he went to get a large popcorn with two sodas. He added some kind of caramel powder to the popcorn. After a taste test to deem it perfect, he carried the tray holding their food in one hand while wrapping the other around her as they went to find their seats.

Going down the hallway to find theater room 4, the movie in the second one must have let out. Lilian spotted a couple of girls from her class laughing as they came through the doors. They spotted her at the same time and stopped talking, stunned. Even though they whispered, Lilian used her wolf hearing to pick up that they were talking about her. How she left class and Dylan had yelled at Chad before following after her.

"She found her mate," the blonde said.

"Poor Alpha to be stuck with her," the brunette replied.

"Why poor Alpha? It's not like we know much about her besides what Chad wants us to think."

"That's true. We'll see what Monday brings."

Monday? Lilian hadn't thought passed today, let alone what Sunday and Monday would bring. Even though she was comfortable with Dylan and felt like they had known each other forever, in reality, it had only been twenty-four hours. She didn't know what the rest of today would be like, let alone Monday. The dreaded Monday. She would have to face her classmates, including Chad, and with no idea what anything would be like now. She knew being a future Luna would get her respect but would it just be faked? Her nervousness wasn't even just about the others but the unpredictability of her pain and if it would be there on Monday.

They passed the girls and found their seats in theater 4. He must have been in tune with her feelings because Dylan sat their tray down on the empty seat to his right. He turned to her, gently grabbing her shoulders, and said, "Don't worry about the girls. Don't worry about Monday. Just think about the here and now with me. We're together now, and it is staying that way. *We* will get through anything, together."

He released her shoulders, placing his arm around her shoulders, letting her cuddle into his side. He handed her a drink for her cupholder, then, after sitting his cup in its place, he held the popcorn between his legs. He grabbed a piece and put it up to her lips. "Have some popcorn, relax, and let's enjoy the movie." She gently took the offered popcorn in her teeth. The sweet and salty taste of caramel on it was surprisingly good.

As the movie started, she helped herself to more, taking turns with Dylan. Halfway through the show, the bucket was empty. That was okay, though. Lilian was comfortable with her head lying on his shoulder, her hand resting on his chest. She enjoyed how it shook his whole body every time he laughed at the movie. It was these little things about him that caused her to love him. A mate bond was definitely strong and helped them have feelings for each other, but it did not force them to feel love. Just Dylan being Dylan was enough for her to have more than sexual attraction, which she was afraid of and didn't want to dwell on.

After the movie finished, they got back in the truck. Lilian could tell they were heading back towards their pack's community, but she was confused when he passed her road up and kept on driving. "Where are we going?"

"A few different places," he told her, smiling at his own secretive reply.

While she couldn't help but smile with him, she was also annoyed. She wasn't one for surprises, and she could already tell she would have to start getting used to them. To try to lose her irritated mood, she rolled down the truck window, letting the wind tease her hair and her worries float away. Not owning a car or a bicycle, or having ever changed into her wolf form, had kept this small act of freedom and joy away from her. She relaxed back into the seat, eyes closed, and her smiling face to the sun, reveling in the moment.

She could feel the truck slowing, the wind now like a gentle feather on her face. She thought about not opening her eyes and pretending to have fallen asleep, but she was too curious. Lilian slowly opened her eyes and stretched a bit. She became alarmed when she realized where they were. "Um, why did you bring me here? I shouldn't be here. Not when everyone thinks of me as a stray." She hid her head below the dash, arms around her in defense.

She could feel the truck as it was placed in park and then turned off. The sound of shifting on the seat caught her attention just before hands gently lifted her up. "You are not a stray, for one. Two, you are with me, which means you are my family. Three, if anyone from your class ever calls you names, teases, or lays their hands on you, they will have me to deal with, including my brother." Dylan usually smiled and joked with her. This protective, fierce side made her feel loved and secure, and she could feel the truth in his words.

While she wanted to shed tears of relief and happiness, she took in some fresh air to clear her head instead. The last thing she needed was for people to see her with a red, tear-stained face and gossip about them. Lilian also didn't want his parents to see her that way. If she were to be Luna, she wouldn't want anyone to see her as weak.

Seeing her calm down, Dylan got out of the truck and walked around to open her door. "You do know that I can open the door, right?" she asked him, smiling and secretly loving this special treatment.

"What kind of gentleman would I be if I didn't open doors for my lady in front of my family?" he playfully replied. He took her by surprise when he lifted her from the seat and kissed her forehead. Then he tucked her into his side, placing his hand on her hip again, and they walked towards the main house. She thought he was staking his claim at the movies doing this, but it hit her harder now that he was doing it in front of pack members, especially his parents and brother.

The house wasn't so much a house, but more of a mansion set at the back of a circle ringed with smaller family homes. The Alpha's family lived in the main home, where others could live if needed, such as when visiting or in emergencies. With such a large pack, its size was well proportioned. There were a few other buildings back here, too, like a small bar and restaurant and the pack store, which they could visit if needed without going back into the main town.

Dylan walked her straight to the main house. Lilian thought it reminded her of an older plantation home because of its size, cottage feel, and wraparound porch. They took the stairs together in sync, as if they had known each other for far longer than they had. He opened the door and motioned for her to go in ahead of him. She walked in and immediately removed her shoes and placed them in the line of shows in front of the entryway bench. There were hooks on the whole wall for coats and hats, but she wasn't wearing one today. Dylan closed the door and slid his shoes off before taking her hand in his and leading the way through the banquet-style dining room and into a large living room.

His family sat on couches watching a movie together. Chad glanced their way and scowled before turning back to the movie. Lilian wondered if he was mad at her for being his brother's mate or at Dylan for embarrassing him at school. *Probably both*, she thought with a sigh. She didn't expect him to like her, but she just hoped there wouldn't be anymore drama.

Noticing Chad's actions, their dad and Alpha Thomas looked over to see Dylan standing in the arched entrance with his arm around Lilian. He nudged Luna Marianne so she would look before they both stood up. "Welcome home, Dylan," greeted Alpha Thomas. "Who do we have here?" he asked, waiting for the introduction.

"Dad. Mom," he started with a nod in greeting to each. "When you sent me to the school with Chad's practice duffle, I finally met my mate. Meet Lilian."

Lilian heard Chad say, "Yeah, meet the stray," under his breath, and her cheeks turned red. She felt ready to run out of there, but Dylan only held her tighter to him.

She wasn't the only one who turned red. The Alpha looked furious, and the Luna looked horrified at their younger son. Before Alpha Thomas could begin to speak, Luna Marianne had already started. "What did you just say?! I've heard things about you from your teachers and principal that I hoped were not true. You just confirmed that they were right. You can go to your room! And do not think about playing any of your electronic games either. If you do, I will remove them all and make you earn each system and each game back." She paused before continuing her be-rating.

"You will *never* call anyone that name ever again, or any name that makes them feel insignificant. You will *never* tease anyone *ever* again. And don't you even think of getting an attitude with me, or Lilian, over this, or else I will have you removed from the football team. Not just from being captain either, because no leader disrespects their people like that. Do you hear me?!"

Chad had never been yelled at or disciplined before, and his face held total shock. Lilian could see his eyes shine with unshed tears as his future on the football team as a senior could be torn away. He was stunned at being reprimanded for bullying Lilian. Chad never saw it as a big deal but more just his own entertain-ment. But now, seeing his mom furious with him had put his actions in a different light. Lilian could see it as the different emotions flashed across his face, from anger toward her, shame in front of his parents, and terrified of any repercussions. With his fists clenched, he went to his room as told. She was surprised when he didn't talk back like he would at school. Maybe at home, he was different.

Dylan cleared his throat as if trying to clear out the tension in the room. When his parents turned back towards him, he asked, "Would you mind if we take this up to your office in case any pack members would come?"

"No, no. Of course, I don't mind. That would have been a better place than here for that, um, discussion that just happened." Alpha Thomas and his wife took the stairs up to the office with Dylan and Lilian left to follow. The Alpha sat at his desk while Luna Marianne sat on an extra chair beside him. After Lilian entered the room, Dylan gently closed the door and showed her to the couch in front of the desk so they could stay beside each other.

Chapter 8

When they were all settled, Dylan didn't wait. He cut to the chase with the question he wanted an answer to most. "Mother, why did you never make sure that Lilian knew about our Center for food, our health insurance options, and anything else that could have benefited her the last five years? She's been barely surviving on a diet of bread, bananas, and ibuprofen."

Luna Marianne looked surprised, but then her expression changed to shame. "At first, I thought she was too young to understand those things. I used to visit her often, but things got busier around here with you and your brother in sports. I guess I forgot to visit once I lost the habit."

"You thought she was too young to know about the Center and insurance, yet she was left to live in a house by herself at twelve years old?"

Luna Marianne looked at Lilian, ashamed with tears in her eyes. "I am so sorry, Lilian," she apologized. "When your father passed away, you had already been looking after yourself for a long time. I should have had you come here to live, where you could have still had your independence but yet help when you needed it. I apologize for you having to struggle needlessly."

Lilian looked at her hands where they lay in her lap, clasped together from nervousness. She softly replied, "It's okay."

"No, dear. It isn't okay. As a Luna, I should be there for all pack members, especially those who need it most. I haven't been there for you, and that is my fault. Whatever you need, we will get it figured out."

"Thank you, Mom," Dylan said. "I'm glad you said that because we need Lilian to be seen by the best doctor we can find around here."

His mom went from looking ashamed to suddenly alert and alarmed. "What's wrong?"

"She's been suffering from horrible pain in her lower abdomen since she was twelve. It is so bad that she has been ignoring the urge to shift for that long because she didn't want her wolf to suffer if it were something that would affect them both. She has this pain throughout the whole month. She's worried that she can't be my mate, Luna, if she can't have any children. She's never been seen because she thought she had no insurance and has suffered from whatever this is alone until you sent me to take Chad his bag. I stayed with her yesterday and through the night to help where I could."

"Son, you are sure she is your mate?" his father asked. "It won't influence what care she gets. I just want to know."

"Yes, Dad. She is definitely my mate. In fact, my wolf was able to help hers stay calm last night when the urge to shift for the moon began."

Alpha Thomas nodded thoughtfully. "I believe you. A wolf mate can definitely work miracles."

"Yeah, like being able to rein in your wild side?" his mom joked.

"That was definitely a miracle." Alpha laughed, and they all chuckled. Then he turned serious and looked at both Dylan and Lilian. "Have you begun to make any plans?"

"We haven't talked about the future much," Dylan confessed. "I want to see her healthy and happy, first and foremost. Once we visit the doctors, then we will work out other details. One thing at a time."

Lilian felt relief. She knew she was his mate, but she didn't know if there would be a future yet. She needed to figure out what was wrong with her first. If she was dying or infertile, she wanted Dylan to be aware before making any permanent decisions about his own future. He might claim he would stick with her, but Lilian knew people that changed their minds throughout her young life. It was still hard to fully trust someone when she was always getting hurt.

The Alpha looked at his son, pride shining in his eyes. "I am proud of you for coming to that decision. It shows your maturity and how serious you are about your mate. I agree. We will make sure she sees a doctor, gets the best treatment, and then we will go from there." Then he turned his gaze on Lilian. "In the meantime, please take what you need, or want, from what is available at the Center and know you are welcome here any time. Okay?"

Lilian nodded, not trusting her voice when faced with how nice the Alpha and Luna were. *Why didn't I ever ask them for help? I knew pack leaders would help their members, yet I never reached out. This situation I'm in isn't just because the Luna quit visiting but because I was trying too hard to be independent and just plain stubborn. Well, stubborn and stupid. I could have had things easier while still being my own person this entire time.* She couldn't help these thoughts from racing through her head. While berating herself, she also felt hopeful and like today was the beginning of a better life.

Dylan took her by the hand, and they stood up together. He led her closer to his father's desk, and the Alpha and Luna shook their hands, acknowledging their unity and support for one another. They all left the room with smiles. The current Alpha and Luna went back to watching their show while Dylan led Lilian outside.

Lilian thought they would go towards his truck, but instead, he turned her away from it. Still holding hands, he walked up a gravel road that went past his parents' home and into the woods. She figured he had a plan and let him guide her as she enjoyed the peaceful walk. Walking was definitely better and easier when she wasn't in one of her pain flares. Today had been a good day so far, but in the back of her mind, she kept questioning when it would be ruined. She couldn't remember the last full day, let alone two days, that she had been pain-free. It didn't help her anxiety to always have it in the back of her mind, either. She was sure that stress increased the flares.

The small road led to an opening in the woods. The cutest cabin she had ever seen was in the middle of that clearing. The lawn was mowed, bushes under the windows were trimmed, and the flowers in the window boxes were still blooming. Dylan led her to the small front porch that was big enough for a swing. He opened the door and let her enter ahead of him.

The inside was just as cute as the outside was. There was a cozy living room with wooden furniture with plush cushions, a glass top table with a wood frame, a stone fireplace with a thick slab wood mantel, and a large television above the fireplace. Behind the living room were the dining room and kitchen that matched in design; wood, with rustic pattern fabrics like plaid, and even a bouquet of flowers on the dining table.

There was a hallway that had four doors. She assumed those were bedrooms and a bathroom.

"What do you think?" Dylan asked her quietly.

"It is beautiful," she replied. "Whoever decorated and landscaped did great. Everything goes together, and I love the quaint charm."

"Well, thank you," he said.

Lilian looked at him with surprise. "You did the decorating?"

"I did," he said with pride. "I built this cabin myself, decorated it, and maintained it."

"Wow! That is incredible," she said, shocked. "I cannot imagine how long it all took, but you did amazing. Do you live here?"

"When I'm not traveling for pack business, I do. I wanted space away from my family but still close in case of an emergency. Let me show you the rest of the house," he offered. He showed her up the hallway and opened each door; three bedrooms, but one looked like an office and had a futon. There was a bathroom, but it was the guest bathroom. Turned out, the master bedroom had its own luxury bath and walk-in closet. The more natural decor and furniture flowed throughout the entire house.

"You have a lot of space," she commented as they stood inside his bedroom.

"Well, I built it, not just for myself, but with my mate and future in mind." He let the comment sink in before asking, "What do you think? Can you see yourself living here? With me?"

Lilian looked him over. His hands were tucked into his pockets, most likely to not fidget from how nervous he looked. *He is so cute right now. Should I tease him a bit? He reminds me of the boys at school asking a girl to prom.* She decided not to. She couldn't be cruel, especially after all he had done for her and how hard she was already falling in love.

"My house has never been a home. It is quiet, bare, and far from being cozy. This place? This house, home, that you built? It is the complete opposite. I could feel the love put into it when we walked up outside. The inside is beautiful and warm, and I don't know if I can even imagine what it would be like staying here. However, I would love to give it a try."

Suddenly, Lilian felt her feet leaving the floor as Dylan picked her up and twirled her around. "You don't know how happy you just made me," he confessed.

Lilian wrapped her legs around his waist and her arms around his neck. She felt his hands support her bottom to keep her from slipping. Seeing the joy in Dylan's eyes, she lowered her head and claimed his smiling mouth in a kiss. She put her love, happiness, gratefulness, and all the other emotions she was feeling into it. Just yesterday, she kissed him for the first time. Heck, kissed anyone for the first time. Now she was initiating the kiss and letting her emotions guide her.

Dylan walked them slowly over to his bed. It was waist-high and perfect for her to sit on while they continued to make out. Lilian let her hands go under his shirt and around his back to hold him close. His own hands held onto her hips. She could feel his need for her growing, and she felt the same need like a curling heat in her usually cursed area. She had never been with anyone before, and because of the pain, she never attempted to explore her own body either. She wanted him, but was nervous. *Will it hurt? Will it cause my pain to return? Am I too inexperienced for him?*

She could tell he was holding back and felt the need to be with her mate, to meet his needs. He broke their kiss, both breathing heavily, and asked breathlessly, "Is this too fast?"

"Probably," she said. "But I feel like I have known you for years, and I know we will have years to come. This isn't just a fling or a one-night stand, right?"

"Right," he echoed.

Lilian wasn't sure what to do or where to put her hands, but she felt ready to find out. She knew sex was a natural part of human, and animal, behavior, so she would embrace it. To prove to him she was ready, Lilian unbuttoned his jeans and lowered the zipper. She could feel him shuffle as he slid his shoes off. She helped raise his shirt up until he quickly tore it off the rest of the way. He returned the favor by helping remove her own shirt as she kicked her shoes off. As he stood back to remove his pants, she laid back and took hers off, leaving herself in just her basic black bra and bikini bottoms.

Out of self-consciousness, she wrapped her arms around her stomach. It wasn't toned like the other girls' bodies, and there were a few stretch marks because of the constant bloating. With his full Adonis body bare, Dylan walked up to her and gently pried her arms away from her. She kept her eyes low in shame, but his aroused cock was vying for her attention as it proudly showed off in her lowered view.

He cupped her chin, raised her head, and said, "You are beautiful. But we don't have to continue if you are uncomfortable."

"I want to," she whispered. "I just don't like my stomach," she admitted, baring her faults and self doubts to him.

"Guess what? I don't like my nose with its lump from breaking it during a football game my senior year of high school. We each have something we are embarrassed about, but guess what? I love your stomach. It is real and shows just how strong you have been."

Lilian had never seen it that way before. Maybe if she tried to see the positives, she would be able to embrace herself more. She wanted to be truly happy and open with Dylan and would do anything to achieve that. "I like your nose because it isn't perfect, and it is you."

"Neither of us is perfect, but you are perfect for me," he proclaimed. Their lips and hands found each other as they solidified their statements by sealing their pact with a long, passionate kiss. Lilian was done with talking and wanted to feel his body against hers.

She broke away and scooted back onto his bed, crawling under the comforter. Dylan stood there wondering what she was up to when a bikini bottom hit him in the face, followed by the matching bra. He caught the bra before it landed and dropped them onto their pile of clothes before quickly climbing into bed next to her.

Under the blankets, neither could see the other's faults nor their own. It helped Lilian feel more secure in herself and free, slightly wild. Her wolf was giving a low growl that vibrated her core, which was already hot and needy, making it build more.

Dylan adjusted the blanket as he rose over her. He must have needed to feel their bodies touch as well. As he leaned down to kiss her, he rested his body on his bent arms so their bodies were together, but he kept most of his weight off her. Wanting more of him, Lilian gripped his thighs and pulled them towards her, so he moved higher. She had seen his cock, but she wanted to feel it under the guise of darkness to sate her curiosity.

She wrapped a hand around him and slid it up and down, feeling the velvety softness opposite of how hard he was. Hard for her. She felt oddly pleased knowing that she had done that to him. She also loved hearing the growl that escaped from him as she felt him. Wanting to learn what else he liked, she cupped his balls and gave a squeeze, releasing another growl. Then she took her fingers and lightly stroked him like a feather, drawing a hiss as he took in air with surprise. *Hmm. I definitely can get used to this,* she thought before he took her hands and held them over her head.

"You have teased me. Now it's my turn," Dylan warned just before he took her mouth to her breast, teeth scraping her beaded nipple and his tongue darting out to lick it. It was her turn to hiss as he bit and teased each one. She was shocked at how it both tickled and stung, yet felt so good. Satisfied her breasts had equal attention, he went lower and kissed her where he remembered seeing her stretch marks to prove he didn't care about them. She whimpered at the sweetness of his actions.

Lilian felt his hand nudging her leg over, bending it at the knee, to open herself up to him. She felt him slide a finger into her, surprised that it went in smoothly and there was no pain yet. Her body was ready for him, but he wanted to make sure her first time was enjoyable. He added another finger to stretch her out for him, her hips moving on their own to ride his hand. He crooked a finger and hit a spot that caused her to gasp from the sudden pleasure.

Dylan rose back up over her, and she could see the smirk on his face, pleased with himself. She felt his cock slide against her; he teased them both by rubbing them together. He leaned over and whispered in her ear, "Are you sure?"

She barely managed to whisper, "Yes." She wanted him, and her body needed him. Lilian almost thought he was leaving her when he moved to the side and reached into his side table. He pulled out a foil wrapper and slid on a condom. She hadn't even thought about protection, and it once again showed her how thoughtful he was. He settled himself back over her and lifted her legs so they wrapped around him. He held her hips up and thrust into her. She felt the sting, being her first time, but he took a few seconds to pause, letting her body adjust to him before he gently began to move. Each gentle thrust rubbed over that sensitive spot he had found before. Each touch increased the warmth she felt and built the pressure until she thought she would explode.

Dylan was also reaching his breaking point and drove in harder and harder, speeding up until hearing Lilian scream out her orgasm. He took that as the cue to let himself go and let his own pleasure roll him. She felt his arms seemingly give out, and he laid down half on top of her and half next to her on the bed. Her leg was pinned under him, but she didn't care. She was still enjoying the feeling of being together, of how he had filled her, taking away the emptiness she had felt for years. His weight felt more like a security blanket than a burden.

When he caught his breath, Dylan got up to use the bathroom. She couldn't help but sigh at the loss. He didn't take long to return to bed, and they lay together. Just like last night, but this time skin to skin. It wasn't even evening yet, but she let herself doze off.

Chapter 9

L ilian was awakened by the largest cramp she had ever had. She must have made noise from the attack her body decided to inflict on her as she curled into a ball out of habit. Dylan wrapped his arms around her to try and comfort her. "What the matter? What can I do?"

"It's a huge cramping pain. It isn't like before. Do you have any ibuprofen? If not, I packed some in my purse out in your truck."

"I have some in the kitchen," he said and tried to get out of bed as gently as he could, afraid that moving the bed could cause her more pain. He knew all his curtains were closed, and the pack never visited his cabin. This allowed him to walk naked to the kitchen to get Lilian some pain relief tablets and water from his refrigerator.

He returned as quickly as possible and helped her sit up. He sat beside her and rested his arm for support as she took the pills and water. She sat the water on the side table and leaned into him while hugging her stomach. "Is there anything else I can do? Would a hot bath help?"

"I've never tried a hot bath. The pack house only has a shower," she told him. "It does sound nice, though."

"If you want to lay back down, I'll get the bath ready," he said as he gave her a gentle squeeze and a kiss on her forehead.

Lilian lay there trying to concentrate on listening to the noise in the bathroom rather than thinking about the pain. She could hear the water pouring to fill the bathtub. That wasn't the sound she was listening to, though. She kept hearing bottles clanking, and it sounded like one must have fallen to the floor. "Shit, my fucking toe!" rang out through the door. She forgot about the pain for a moment as she couldn't help but laugh loudly.

Dylan came to the doorway and peeked at her, "Oh, so you think that was funny? I'm in here fixing up the bath, and you laugh at me getting hurt. Really?"

Lilian was still laughing and answered, "Yup! Definitely laughing."

"I love your laugh, but please don't tell me I have to hurt myself to hear it every time," he joked.

"I mean, it could help." She shrugged.

He smiled as he shook his head. "Damn, I love you," he said before ducking back into the bathroom. *Wait, did he just say what I think he said? Sure, we are mates, and we had sex. Isn't it too early for those words?* Lilian didn't know how to respond. This was the first time she could remember hearing them, and she felt awkward.

She was still lying there quietly when Dylan came back out. He stood beside the bed and said, "Don't worry about needing to say that back to me yet. It just felt like the right time for me, and I couldn't help it." He reached down and swept her up into his arms.

"Do you like carrying me or something? I could have tried walking."

"You could, but if I can save you from any pain, I will. Just think of this as me getting in practice for carrying you over the threshold in our future," he said, lightly joking while being serious.

When Dylan gave her a tour earlier, they never entered the master bath. It was about the size of her own bedroom, and calling the large soaker tub with jets a bathtub was a complete understatement. It even had a standalone shower big enough for five people beside it. Her nose picked up on some different scents. Did he add oils besides bubble bath? No wonder it sounded like he was mixing a magic potion before.

He gently laid her in the giant tub, the water so deep it went up to her neck, stinging but feeling great.

"How do you feel?"

"This is the first time I can actually say that I feel like a princess, or at least how I think they would feel. You have been pampering me and spoiling me, and I feel like I have done nothing for you," she confessed.

"Having you in my life is all I need. You by my side spoils me. I know we will have rough patches, but for now, I just want to experience our newfound relationship to its fullest. Plus, I feel like I have to make up for my family's neglect," he told her, covering her lips with his finger so she wouldn't deny it. "Ouch! Did you actually just bite my finger?"

"Well, you put your finger by my mouth and tried to shut me up. So yes, yes I did," she said smugly.

"Feisty," he teased. "I like it!"

Lilian rolled her eyes at his playfulness. While she loved it, she wasn't going to let him know that. "You know, if you are going to stay in here naked while I'm in here, you might as well get in too. It's not like this bath isn't big enough. Probably could fit three people," she joked.

"If I didn't want to keep my mate to myself, I probably could call Dan to test that theory. I'd rather keep you to myself," he said as he climbed into the tub on the opposite side. "I don't know the last time I laid in here. I'm usually in a rush and just take quick showers. It actually feels nice," he admitted.

Lilian watched as he laid his head back on the edge of the tub, eyes closed. She looked at the bubbles all around them and couldn't help it. She slowly shifted in the tub, gathered up a handful, and piled them onto his face before he could realize what was happening. He began to sputter as he got the taste in his mouth. With a smile, he moved the bubbles down to his chin. "Do I look good with a beard?"

She giggled. "Only if you are trying to be Santa with that white fuzz," she teased back. Her stomach decided that was when it would let them both know that it was hungry, and it wasn't happy with just the pills. "I guess that means I need to get washed up." She laughed.

Dylan reached behind him where he had towels and tossed her a cloth while holding onto his. Lilian was jealous of how fast he could wash up. He was done before she had even started on her hair! "Would you rather wash your hair in the shower?" he asked. Not sure if rinsing with bubble bath would be good for your hair." He stepped out onto the plush mat lying by the tub and then walked into the shower to turn on the water to let it warm up for her.

Lilian watched in awe as he showed a level of thoughtfulness she had never known or experienced. Dylan was really opening up her eyes to a completely different life. She had known neglect and loneliness, yet in just over twenty-four hours, he snuck his way into her heart and showed her what love and consideration were. *Will I ever get used to this, or will I always be making comparisons?* She gave herself a mental shake before getting out of the tub, flipping the toggle on her way out to let the water drain. The cool air hit her and made her dash for the warmth of the shower. Dylan let her in, and he stepped out. "Not staying?" she asked.

"If I stay, I don't think I can stop myself from physically showing how much I'm attracted to you," he sheepishly confessed. "But take your time while I go and start cooking supper. I feel like I could eat a whole buffet," he joked.

Lilian watched as he left the room wrapped in a bath towel. She wondered if she would find him still naked in the kitchen if she hurried. While she still could feel the twinge of a cramp, it was way better than before. The slight pain wasn't enough to distract her from her dirty thoughts. The vision of him naked and cooking a big juicy steak was enough to make her rush with her hair and brave the chill of leaving the shower.

She stepped into the room and spotted her clothes on the floor near the bed. The idea of putting them back on made her crinkle her nose. She had a feeling that Dylan would want to stay here for the night, an idea she wasn't opposed to at all. His place seemed more like a home than the one she spent the whole eighteen years of her life in with all its bad memories. Dylan claimed her as his mate in front of his parents, so it would be safe to assume this was her home now.

So why shouldn't she get comfortable? She spotted his wardrobe across the room and walked quickly to it in case he would be coming. She opened the doors wide, rifled through his shirts to find just a plain tee, and slipped it on. It was long enough to cover her butt in case of company, which was a good thing since she didn't have an extra pair of underwear.

She quietly tiptoed down the hallway towards the kitchen, stood at the entrance, and leaned on the wall. She found that she loved watching Dylan cook. Maybe someday she would ask him to help teach her so they could cook together, but for now, she was entertained by being on the sidelines. Dylan seemed in his element when he cooked. He glided from the refrigerator to the counter and the stove. A little seasoning there, a flip here, taste, and repeat until his nod of approval. It was like watching a dance. Each move was perfect, rhythmic, and with total self-confidence. *Who knew I would find this so damn hot? I wonder if I would enjoy watching cooking or dancing shows...*

He continued finishing up creating his masterpiece supper, totally focused and not realizing she was there. She watched as he plated up freshly made mashed potatoes, medium rare steak, and mushroom gravy over the top. *How did he know that I was daydreaming about steak? Well, I pictured him naked and not in a different pair of flannel pajama pants and a tank top. But they will do,* she thought as they were well fitted on his butt, which she was currently admiring.

He carried the plates to the dining table, where she noticed there were now lit candles beside the flowers from earlier. *He already has my heart in his hands yet still adds romantic little touches to make me melt even more.* Lilian couldn't believe that he was hers.

Maybe the Moon Goddess felt she deserved the sweetness of this Alpha's love and care after trying so hard to survive by herself. The Moon Goddess was the one that determined who was fated mates. However, each of her wolves was also given free will as to whether they would accept or reject those bonds. Lilian still couldn't stop thinking that Dylan wanting to keep her was anything short of a miracle. She knew how Dylan saw her. She just needed to work on how she saw herself. Maybe then she would feel worthy and equal, because if she couldn't see it, how would the rest of the pack be able to?

Dylan looked up from where he had just placed the silverware by the plates, finally noticing her standing there. "Have you been there long?" he asked, his cheeks tinted red as he blushed.

"Hmm, maybe ten or fifteen minutes. I couldn't help but watch you cook and think how lucky I am to be here with you."

He walked over to her and caressed her face with his hands as he gave her a quick kiss. "That's funny because I keep thinking I am the lucky one." He took her by the hand and pulled her towards the table, even pulling her chair out. She sat down and adjusted the chair closer before starting to eat. The steak was tender enough that she could cut through it with her fork. They ate in silence as Lilian savored every bite, and her craving for steak was finally sated.

When their forks clanked on the empty plates, Dylan asked, "Are you tired, or would you like to watch something on tv?"

"I think watching movies with you is my official new favorite pastime," Lilian admitted. She stood up and grabbed the plates before he could this time. He tried to voice his opinion, but she told him, "You cooked and did the dishes this morning, and you cooked tonight. I think I can take care of the dishes for once. Why don't you go pick the movie, and I'll join you in a few minutes?" Deciding that she was being fair, he went along with her and went to find something to watch.

It wasn't often that she washed dishes. Bananas didn't require a fork; all toast sometimes needed was a butter knife, if she even had peanut butter. She noticed a sponge on the end of a dish wand and decided to try it out. The soap in the handle dispensed through the sponge, making the task easier and faster than she remembered dishes ever going. It also helped that there wasn't grease in the pan and food wasn't dried on the plates. If Dylan always cooked for himself, she could see the advantage of keeping up with the dishes. *Maybe I can be a decent housewife,* she thought.

Lilian finished up in the kitchen and went to join Dylan on the couch. The wooden frame made her think it wouldn't be comfortable, but the plush futon cushion was surprisingly soft and thick. The first movie they watched was a rom-com, and she sat cuddled into his side. The next one was a country western romance, and they laid down, spooning on the couch, to enjoy the calmness of the show. So calm, in fact,

Lilian dozed off, and rather than move her, Dylan stayed where he was too and slept the night away.

Chapter 10

They were sitting down eating breakfast together when Lilian decided to try asking if he had plans for the day already.

"Depends on your thoughts," he eluded.

"My thoughts?"

"Yeah. Do you like it here or want to go back to your place?"

"I don't see that place as mine. It's a pack house. This place you built with your own hands is warmer and feels more like home than that house ever has," she said, speaking the truth.

"Then the question is, do you want to live here?"

"You mean, move in?" she asked. While she wasn't fully surprised, she didn't expect that option for a while. *Is it bad that I feel... relief? Happiness?*

Dylan gave her a nod to confirm her question was the right interpretation. "Yes, I mean move in. Live here with me?" He cleared his throat and drank his orange juice to try and hide his nervousness as he waited for her answer.

"Yes, I will," she said. *Why not?* she thought. *I know I love him. My life has already changed for the better tenfold. Why not just jump in the deep end and learn how to swim together?*

"Do you want to go and pack up, or would you prefer if Dan grabs everything for you? Whichever makes you comfortable."

"Would he mind? I don't have much there. It's mainly just the clothes in the dresser, my school bag, and the textbooks on the desk."

"No knick knacks or pictures?"

"Nothing that I want. Any of those either belonged to my dad or hold memories I don't want to see anymore. Just the main things I want. I can get anything else from the Center, now that I know about it."

"I respect that," he told her. "I will call Daniel in a bit. In the meantime, is there anything you want to do today?"

"Oh, are you asking me for plans now?" she teased.

He actually managed to look sheepish when he said, "I only had yesterday planned. Last night? That was spontaneous, and I loved it. Having you here made it feel like a true home."

"Maybe you could go with me to the center, and you can show me around the pack village?" Lilian couldn't help but sigh with her next thought. "Then I guess I must do homework and prepare for whatever Monday has in store."

"You know, we have internet out here, and we can get a laptop for you if you would rather finish up school online. If going to the physical school is a nightmare for you mentally, and with your pain being random, it is another option."

"I could really do that? Have my own laptop and go to school from here?" She had never thought about it before. The school library was the place she used computers for homework assignments. She didn't have her own and certainly couldn't afford the internet, so online schooling was never an option. She didn't have true friends at school, and who knew if Chad would hold a grudge and try to get back at her or not? She might miss a couple of teachers, but online would give her the flexibility to see doctors too.

Dylan chuckled at the astonishment and joy that lit up her face. It looked as if she had been handed a mountain of gold. "When we visit the center, we will see what they have for laptops, and if you don't like any of them, we can go into Luna Cove to shop around."

"I don't have any money to shop," she admitted.

"Remember when you said you felt I was treating you like a princess?" he asked. Lilian nodded so he could continue. "Well, you are the Luna to my Alpha and soon to the pack. My mom is the current Luna, and like the Queen of our pack, if you will, that would make you the Princess Luna. We all have access to the pack's money and can use it for things we need. We all work and contribute to the pack fund, and someday, you will too."

"Everyone works? Even you?" Lilian couldn't help but ask. He had stayed with her since Friday, and she never saw or heard anything about a job. Besides his traveling for pack business, this was the first time he mentioned it.

"I work," he nodded. "I work mostly online because I can take work with me when I travel for pack business. My parents have a few vacation homes they rent out to people. I manage the schedules and the staff that clean and maintain them. My mom takes care of the accounting and billing while my father runs this pack and watches for any more places he can invest in."

"Wow. I never knew your parents did all that. I just assumed they lived like a king and queen where they managed our pack, and that's how they stayed in the house and earned money."

"Many don't know about their investment adventures since the places are out among the humans and not around Luna Cove. I think many do view them as royalty like you did. They haven't spoken out against that image, so I haven't either. It's a bit fun having that secret and something to fall back on if the need would arise."

Lilian didn't want to think about what needs those would be to cause them to give up the Alpha house. She had a feeling that anything that could lose them their home would be devastatingly bad for us all. "I can't wait until I can help and work. If I can find something online after I finish my schooling, maybe I can handle it," she mused out loud. "I'm actually really excited about all these changes and possibilities that you are giving me." Tears started welling up in her eyes.

Dylan got up and crouched beside her to give her a hug. "I told you we would get through this all together. You are my mate, and I will do anything I can to make you happy. You know that, right?"

Lilian sniffled and gave a little nod. "These are just happy tears. I never saw anything like this in my future. Heck, I never pictured a future for myself until you swept into my life."

"And it will be a great one," he added. "I think your clothes should be done in the dryer. If you want to get ready to go to the center, I'll call Dan and then get ready myself."

Still sniffling, Lilian stood up as Dylan was clearing their plates. She couldn't help but shake her head and laugh a bit. *Of course he would tell me to go and take care of my clothes, because why wouldn't he? He never wants help with the dishes.*

Before breakfast, he had shown her where the laundry room was, off the kitchen, just before entering the attached garage. He told her that although he loved her wearing his shirt, it might not be public-friendly, and he didn't want other guys staring at her. The thought that other guys would stare at her with any form of interest made Lilian laugh, but she still washed her clothes. Until Dan brought her other ones, this outfit would have to work. She took them out of the dryer, still nice and warm, and went to the master bathroom to get ready.

She splashed water on her face and then used her fingers to comb through her hair and brush her teeth with some toothpaste. Dylan, unfortunately, didn't need a brush, and she didn't trust his comb to not get stuck in her hair. She also didn't know if he was picky about sharing his toothbrush and didn't want to test it. Her fingers worked well enough for now. She would have to remember to get the essentials and not let the excitement over a laptop take over.

As Lilian walked out of the bathroom, she spotted Dylan sitting on the bed waiting, clothes already changed. "Ready to go?" he asked.

"I think so," she told him. "I can't wait to see the center and all there is."

"You will probably be in shock," he joked. "I'll finish getting ready in the bathroom if you want to wait in the living room."

She gave him a quick smile before leaving the room quickly. While she would have loved to admire him as he got ready, she was too excited and wanted to do anything she could to move things along. He must have known how anxious she was because she didn't even sit down before he opened the front door for her. "Lead the way," he told her, waving a hand like he was displaying the outside. Lilian gave him a little giggle before she skipped out the door. Dylan grabbed his keys and wallet from the stand near the door, locked up, and then ran to catch up to her.

"You must be feeling pretty good today," he remarked as they jogged side by side.

"I am," she said. "I know stress can cause some of the pain flares. Just being with you, having food to eat, knowing I can see a doctor, and looking forward to online school have taken most of my stressors away. I do have some pain, mostly near my hip joints, but it is manageable. I've had pain for so long that even just having it lessen feels great."

"I can see how it would feel better. I'm just thankful to the Moon Goddess that she let me find you when I did. Being near you calms my inner wolf, and I love caring for you. It's made me less lonely and grumpy."

"Grumpy? I don't think you can manage that one," she said. He always showed her a smile, concern, humor, and patience. The good emotions. "Not once have I seen you grumpy yet, just upset and protective when you caught Chad in class."

"After living and traveling for business alone, things get redundant and boring, which can turn me into a grouch. You have made things interesting for me again." They both slowed down as they neared the end of his driveway and the opening of the pack village. Walking slowly, Dylan put his arm around her in the now familiar way. Lilian leaned into his shoulder and threaded her fingers through his hand resting on her hip. Now that she was getting more comfortable with his way of claiming her, she wanted to show that she claimed him back. Her arm that was tucked beneath his wrapped around his back, and they walked as one towards the large shed-like building labeled Center on its sign.

Dylan let her go in first, and Lilian barely took five steps before stopping in amazement. From the outside, the building looked small and simple, but inside it looked like there was a little of everything; aisles of essential supplies, coolers, and shelves full of food, racks of clothes towards the back, and a corner with electronic displays. "Wow," she said in awe. "It's like a mini supermarket!"

Dylan leaned over and whispered, "Except here, when you checkout, everything rings up zero."

"I don't believe that yet."

"You will," he said with a smirk.

"If everything rings up zero, then why take things through a checkout?" she retorted.

"So the manager, Ellen, can keep track of the inventory and know when to order more things. She can also see how much of each item 'sells' to determine how popular something is and if she should get rid of it or stock up." Lilian just nodded in response as she thought it over. She could see how keeping track of 'sales' could help. That way, only needed things were there using up the space. Interesting.

"Why don't you take a cart and just start browsing for what you need while I look at the groceries?" he offered. "What would you like for dinner?"

"How about pizza to go with another movie?"

"You got it! I'll gather the ingredients while you shop and find you when I'm finished." She smiled as he grabbed his cart and headed straight to the food.

I wonder whether all guys get excited about food shopping or if it's just a Dylan thing. Shaking her head, she took her own cart and started with the hygiene things, remembering needing a new hairbrush and toothbrush. *I should probably get a razor to shave my legs,* she thought as she didn't think guys found hairy legs sexy.

Oooh, they have different feminine pad sizes! Better get a box of each. With her cycle never being the same, she never knew what she would need. Sometimes she needed overnights during the day, while other times, it was just spotting. Going anywhere during that week was a gamble. She also grabbed more pain relievers since she didn't know what Dylan had left. Ibuprofen, migraine relief, Tylenol, sinus meds, peppermint tea, and gas relief pills. *Geesh, I'm stocking a whole medicine cabinet,* she thought with a laugh. *Better to be prepared than not!*

Migraine relief seemed to help with other pain relievers. She had heard once that the caffeine in them helped the rest work better, like it gave ibuprofen energy or something. The peppermint tea sometimes helped with the bloating, while the Gas X was for, well, gas. Sometimes the inflammation from pain flares would spread into her head and make her eyes ache, and the sinus meds would lessen the pressure. While the items seemed random, each one had its purpose, and Lilian was just thankful she could have them handy now.

Looking through the rest of the essential aisle, she grabbed some non-man shampoo, conditioner, body wash, and a small bottle of perfume. Her eyes widened when she spotted the medical supply zone. She beelined it for a heating pad. Looking around to make sure she was alone, she let herself hug the box. She had never had one and could just picture being able to use it whenever she needed to. Something so small to most others was very precious to her. Looking at the treasures in her cart, she felt like she was rich, being able to get anything she needed and wanted.

When she thought she had her needs filled, she went to the clothes. Dan wasn't going to find much to bring back as she had only one coat, a sweatshirt, and just one dresser drawer full of decent but worn clothes. Lilian helped herself to new undergarments, shoes, tee shirts, jeans, and a couple nightgowns. She also slipped in a lacey nightgown and a matching blouse and skirt. *Something nice for Dylan and something nice for me when we go out,* she decided.

Of course, Dylan would have perfect timing. As soon as something sexy was in the cart, he came around with his cart to peek at what she had found. He couldn't help but raise an eyebrow at her and give her a little sly smile. *Who knew a smile like that would turn my insides into molten lava?* she thought. What a new feeling, and not all that unpleasant...

"Ready to take a look at the laptops and anything else over there?" he asked.

"Anything else?" she asked him, perplexed.

"I did say you could get anything. You aren't limited to a laptop if you don't want to be. Do you want a cell phone? A game console? Television in the bedroom?" he asked, listing everything she had never considered for herself and was always jealous of others over. Knowing that she could have come here the last five years but wasn't aware of it helped her feel better about taking so much. After this trip, she wouldn't need much later on, at least.

Still, in the money-poor mentality, she tried picking out the least expensive options for each item Dylan had listed. However, he wouldn't let her do that. "We owe you for the neglect the last five years. Please, let's get you what you need *and* want." She couldn't think of a response that didn't involve crying, so she nodded and let him help her choose.

"You will need a reliable laptop for your schooling and later if you decide to work from home. If we travel, it would be great for you to have a cell phone in case we need to talk to each other, my parents, or even just to use apps for entertainment." She knew he was explaining these things to give her reasons to not feel bad, but they did help and her tears dried up.

With her cart full and Dylan's approval that she had everything, they went through the checkout. She shook her head in disbelief seeing everything ring up as zero. He did tell her but seeing it actually happening was still shocking. When they were done, Dylan took most of the bags, and Lilian took the rest. "Thank you, Sara," he said to the cashier as she held the door open for them to lug everything out.

They were loading everything into the truck so he could drive it to his place when they heard his mom yelling from the porch. Placing the last bags in, Lilian went to stand beside Dylan and watched as Luna Marianne quickly walked across her lawn to where they were standing. "I am so glad I caught you! I have some news for you, Lilian," she told her. "I made some phone calls and have an appointment for you set up for tomorrow afternoon in Luna Cove with a women's specialist."

"Already?" Lilian couldn't help but ask, speechless again. *Is being speechless going to be my new chronic problem?* she mused.

"I know it's only Sunday, and we only talked yesterday, but after five years, I felt you had dealt with the pain for far too long. I used my contacts to find a specialist who is actually a shifter herself and would know best what to do next. This way, you won't feel the need to hide anything like we would with a typical human doctor."

"Wow, Mom," Dylan said, impressed with what his mom achieved in such a short amount of time. He gave his mom a hug in thanks, and Lilian did as well. "Mom, you never cease to amaze me," he told her. Lilian watched as the Luna's face broke out in a genuine smile, beaming from his praise. *I have a feeling that she doesn't get complimented or recognized for all she does that often. It must be lonely being the Luna and having older sons that don't need her as much. I'll need to remember that for later.* She filed that away in her future to-do list as the Luna gracefully glided back across the yard to her home.

"She is amazing," Lilian said out loud.

"I agree. I sometimes forget, but it's moments like these when I am very grateful to call her Mom." He turned around and gave her a smile. "So. Are you ready to go home?"

"Home. Yet another word that I have to get used to," she admitted as she walked back around to the passenger side and climbed up in. "Yes. Let's go home."

Chapter 11

D ylan's hand rested on her leg that couldn't stop bouncing. "Are you alright?" he asked.

"I will be," Lilian replied. "I've been living with pain for years, yet today just seems like this is so sudden. I'm afraid of the answers but also hopeful. My mind is just overwhelmed."

He placed his arm around Lilian to hug her from the side. It was awkward with the chair arms in between them. Then again, trying to show comfort and affection in the hospital was always an uncomfortable time. "I'll be with you the whole time, unless you need me to step out. Whatever you find out, we'll get through it. You have been strong and independent for years, and you will be for even more to come." Lilian nodded and rested her head on his shoulder.

"Lilian?" a nurse called out.

Lilian gave a slight wave, and they stood up. Dylan gave her another gentle squeeze as they walked over to the nurse and the door leading to the long consultation room hallway. The nurse got her height and weight before showing them into a room with a large monitor. "Unfortunately, your doctor wasn't able to fly in yet on such short notice, but most of the appointment is going over your health and any issues you can think of. You will chat via an online meeting, and your doctor will tell us if you need any tests run before you leave and what your next steps are. I hope that is okay?"

"That's perfectly fine," Lilian said. In fact, without the doctor being there in person, she was a little less nervous. She knew that it meant only a consultation, and anything major would come later, giving her more time to prepare. Before starting their online meeting, the nurse took her vitals and put them into her computer records. Once the doctor was on the screen, she excused herself and left the three of them to talk.

"Hello, I'm Dr. Johnson," she introduced herself. Dr. Johnson had dark hair pulled into a bun and brown eyes. It was hard to tell if her hair was brown or black on the screen. Lilian had to stop looking at the doctor's features and concentrate on the appointment itself. *It isn't like hair color determines experience,* she thought.

"I'm Lilian and this is my mate Dylan," she responded. She wanted to say boyfriend, but with the doctor being a shifter, she would understand the importance of the mate term.

"Lilian, are you comfortable talking about everything with Dylan present?"

"Yes, Doctor. I've told him most of it anyway."

Dr. Johnson nodded. "Well then. Let's get started. When did you have your first menstrual cycle, and did you have pain then?" Lilian told her how it began when she was twelve and that she thought the pain was normal. She mentioned not having her parents for guidance and wasn't aware of having any form of medical insurance, so she toughed it out for the next five years. Dylan prompted her to mention how she always held back from shifting due to her fears about her wolf suffering too. Lilian also mentioned the odd bloating and random pains throughout the month instead of just during her cycle. She then admitted, embarrassed, that after having her first intercourse, she woke up with severe pain a few hours later.

The doctor went on to ask her about other possible symptoms like if she ever was nauseous during a pain flare, got migraines, had digestive issues, and if she felt fatigued. "I never associated those things with my reproductive pain, but yes. I have experienced all of those," Lilian said in surprise.

Dr. Johnson kept typing up notes. When she finished, she looked at Lilian through the camera and asked, "Have you ever heard of endometriosis?"

"That was one of the medical possibilities I found when researching at the school library. Of course, Dr. Internet also threw in cancer like it always does and freaked me out."

"Did you read up on endo much?"

"I did read the symptoms and possible treatments. Some of the medicines seemed scarier than the endo with all their side effects, so I looked up the other treatments more."

Dr. Johnson agreed. "The only way to officially diagnose and treat endo is through laparoscopic surgery to find it and remove any that is found by excision. Basically, that means a few small incisions so we can go in with a camera and tools to cut and endo tissue out. It is surgery, so there would be recovery time, but if you have confirmed endo and we can remove it all, you could have a better quality of life."

Lilian nodded. She had come across that information in a social media information group called Nancy's Nook, knew surgery was the number one treatment, and was glad her doctor mentioned that first. Through Nook, she recognized that was a sign of a knowledgeable specialist, and she could trust her more. "Until we schedule you for surgery, would you like to try some medicine to help with the pain? We could try norethindrone, which doesn't have too many possible side effects. This way, you could try your first shift if it works. Until you shift, we won't know how your wolf is affected since there aren't many records about shifters with endometriosis.

"I'm sure there are more out there that have it, but many just keep hiding the pain because they don't want to seem different from their peers. If more like you were to come forward, the others wouldn't feel as alone, and we could have better information. However, the medicine and shifting are up to you. I won't pressure you on those. For now, I do want you to have some blood work done since you haven't been to the doctor for a long time, and an ultrasound just to get some measurements."

Lilian took a minute to think and Dylan sat quietly to allow her to make her own decisions. "I think I do want to try the meds and the shift. I have wanted to but have been scared. If it might help others for me to find out, then I am more than willing to try."

"All right. I will send the prescription to the hospital's pharmacy and get the tests ordered. You should be able to go to the lab right after our meeting to start the bloodwork, but the ultrasound will probably have to be scheduled. We will also call you back with a surgery date once I look at my schedule and see when I can fly from here in Florida to Wisconsin. Have any more questions?" Lilian shook her head, smiling now that she had a course of action. "Then I will let your nurse know we are finished, and she will help with the rest. Just stay there, and she will be with you in a moment," Dr. Johnson told them, and then the screen went blank.

As soon as the doctor disappeared, Lilian couldn't help but say, "Oh my Goddess. I can't believe it. I have a doctor who listened, a plan, and medicine to try. Am I just dreaming and going to wake up any second?"

"Don't forget, she also gave you permission to shift," Dylan reminded her.

"Should I be afraid? Does it hurt?" Before, Lilian was worried that her wolf might hurt from the same pain that afflicted her. Now she was afraid that shifting would hurt. *How ironic is that?* she questioned herself.

"I think the first time for me was a bit uncomfortable, but it doesn't hurt," he said.

The nurse took that moment to knock on the door and peek her head in. "Are you ready to go? First, let's get the labs done, and then we can fit you in for that ultrasound. Our technician isn't as busy today as she normally is and said she could fit you in between appointments."

Lilian took in a breath and let it out slowly. "Everything is moving so fast. I love being able to get it all done, but it is a bit overwhelming."

"I'll be with you if you want to hold my hand," Dylan said. Lilian gave him a quick smile and then followed the nurse.

The lab filled around six vials of her blood before letting her go on to the ultrasound. She had no idea what all the blood tests were but figured her doctor would know best, and she would find out soon enough. Lilian was more nervous about the scan than the tests. She hadn't been to the doctor in years and never had a yearly physical or pap smear. Luckily, the tech could tell she was nervous and explained the entire process.

First, Lilian needed to put on a hospital gown. Then some cold goop was placed on her stomach so the ultrasound scanner could look at her abdomen from the outside. The tech found one of her ovaries and her uterus. She commented on her uterine wall being thicker than usual and how she couldn't see the other ovary. The tech tried reassuring her by saying that it sometimes happened and neither was too worrisome. After the external scan, the tech had her use the bathroom before she could do the internal exam.

Lilian couldn't believe the pain the internal scan wand caused. Tears welled up as she tried to hold still while the tech quickly took the necessary measurements. She heard the tech say her uterus was retroverted, but she didn't know what that meant. She also couldn't concentrate enough to ask and hoped she would remember to ask Dr. Johnson.

When the tech finished, she completed the scan file on the ultrasound machine and left the room. Lilian was allowed to clean herself up and get dressed in her regular clothes then she could leave when ready. Lilian moaned when she bent to pick up her clothes from the floor. Dylan had her sit down and then got them for her. She was able to put on her bra and shirt, but he helped her with her underwear and pants.

"Let's get your medicine from the pharmacy and then go home. We'll get you some ibuprofen and then watch a movie?" Lilian bit her lip to stop crying and nodded. This time he put his arm around her more to help support her than to be protective.

They managed to get her medicine and home to rest fairly quickly. Lilian was even more grateful to have Dylan's help today. She couldn't imagine going through it alone like she knew some had in that endo group. Yes, Lilian was happy to have answers, but she had only known the medical process and not the physical toll it could take. She was also thankful the full moon had just passed and wouldn't be here for a few weeks. Maybe she could relax a bit before then and try to prepare for it. For now, Lilian just wanted to lay on the couch in Dylan's arms and wait to see if the pills would work.

Chapter 12

The rest of October seemed to pass quickly. The medicine Dr. Johnson prescribed helped her feel more normal. She certainly had less pain and could almost forget she might have endometriosis if it weren't for the small, random twinges where she would normally feel cramps. The pills also stopped her from having her cycle so far.

Lilian was getting used to waking up happy, eating breakfast with Dylan, and then they would spend the day working side-by-side in his office. He would work on managing his parents' rental properties while she was taking her online classes. There were no bullies to cause her to lose focus, and she found she could get through the lessons quickly. Getting ahead on them was a good thing since she had gotten a phone call letting her know her surgery would be happening in mid-November, just before Thanksgiving.

Dylan would be taking a couple days to attend some pack meetings in a different state. Lilian wasn't looking forward to being alone while he was gone, but she would try to keep busy and hope that time passed quickly. She could visit Luna Marianne and the center if she got bored. At least now she had options while alone. Before, the quiet of the old pack house seemed to encourage her depressing thoughts. Her depression and anxiety were lessened by being near her mate. She loved being able to experience happiness, joy, and love when once, she didn't know if those feelings really existed. Less than one month, and her whole life had been flipped upside down. Or was that right side up?

Before Dylan had to leave, he would be with her to get through this upcoming full moon. He told her that he wanted to experience her first time with her. See her wolf and let their wolves meet each other and run free in the woods behind their home. Lilian often tried to picture what it would be like. She was still nervous there would be pain, but she was looking forward to it because she could feel her own wolf's excitement.

Taking a small break from emails, Dylan looked over at her. "Are you ready for tonight?"

"What's tonight?" she asked.

"The full moon that you've been waiting for?"

"Wait. Already?"

"Yes," he said with a laugh. "Already. You will be able to give in to the shift and see how your wolf is. Then, after this shift, you will know how it feels and can shift anytime you want just by recreating that feeling."

"Can we? I've only heard of the moon parties and assumed that was the only time we could shift."

"Nope, we can shift anytime we want. Most just use the full moon to party, or hang out together, while giving into the moon's pull. If you ever feel like you are in danger, or even just bored, you can shift and go for a run."

"That's great to know," she said as she took a mental note. *Is there anything else I don't know or understand about myself?* Dylan was raised around caring parents who could teach him all things shifter. Most days, Lilian felt like a human with an extra personality, her wolf. "Is there anything else I wouldn't know about being a shifter?" she asked him.

"Hmm. I'm not sure," Dylan admitted. "The only things that I can think of would be that shifting can speed up healing, clothes may or may not disappear into the Ether if you change while wearing them, and that silver doesn't actually hurt us. Well, unless it's a bullet because those hurt anyone," he joked. Lilian did give him a little laugh while she thought about how tonight would go. She tried to focus on her schoolwork, but it was harder now with that in the back of her mind.

The afternoon quickly turned to evening. They had eaten dinner and almost finished a movie when Lilian started to feel her wolf stretch out. It felt like her wolf was practicing yoga to get ready. *Downward dog?* she asked her. Lilian could visualize her wolf crooking her head sideways to look at her in the same way a dog looks at their human when they are confused or calling their human stupid. She couldn't help but laugh.

"Is something amusing?" Dylan asked. They were watching a horror movie so for her to laugh was curious.

She tried to explain to him what she felt her wolf was doing, but she couldn't stop giggling. It didn't help that the stretching was also tickling her. *At least I'm entertaining Dylan,* she thought between fits. He turned off the movie to watch her instead.

"Don't worry. My wolf thinks I'm odd all the time, too," he admitted. "Let's close up here and go outside. I think your wolf is just telling you she is impatient with you."

"I think you are right," she tried saying, still giggling. Her wolf wouldn't stop tickling her anytime soon unless she let her have her night.

Dylan helped her stand up, and they walked outside. He closed the door behind her and showed her around to the back of the cabin. This put them next to the woods and made it seem a little more private for her first change. She could hear laughing and shouting coming from the house parties near his parents' house. Those people were all preoccupied with drinking until their midnight shift, so she didn't have to be nervous that they would see her. *What if I change back*

and my clothes don't reappear? That would be horrible
if anyone else was around. Oh, great. Now I have that
to worry about.

"So, how do I do this?" she asked Dylan.

"You just let yourself go and feel your wolf. Give
her permission to take over, and she will," he said in
a matter-of-fact tone.

"That's it?"

"That's it. Then when she's had enough time to
run, you can tell her it's time to change back. You
think about what it's like to feel human, and then you
will turn back. Just remember to picture yourself in
clothes." He laughed.

"Well. Okay then. Here goes nothing," Lilian said,
shaking her arms out to try and lose the nerves. She
gave her wolf the mental nod of approval. *It's your*
time, girl. Let's give this a try. Her wolf gave a big
stretch, and then it felt like she was running. Running
to jump right out of Lilian's body. Lilian was afraid
that her wolf was going to run into a wall, but instead,
when she reached the edge of darkness, Lilian could
see her body begin to blur. It blurred into what must
be the Ether. She felt herself sink into the back of her
wolf's mind as they switched control. It surprised her

how quick and painless the transition was. She felt stupid for not letting it happen sooner.

Her wolf's personality was more prominent now as the wolf instincts were now in control. Lilian could sense the desire to run, the longing to chase after a squirrel she could smell and hear just a hundred yards away, and the need to hunt for food. There was also another feeling. Warmth and the wolf's tail twitched back and forth. Teasing Dylan's wolf? *Oh, you whore,* Lilian teased her. Her wolf gave her an amused feeling. *Yeah, yeah. I am too.* She couldn't help but agree. Dylan made her feel everything with his kindness and attractive body.

Her wolf turned around just as Dylan was letting his own wolf takeover. She watched as his body blurred and a wolf came into view. His was more black while hers greyer. Both had the coloring of a timber wolf, considered local for their region in Wisconsin. When his wolf was fully in control, Lilian watched through her wolf's eyes as he slowly walked near her. He went behind her and began sniffing her. Her wolf felt his paw at her back, as if seeking permission, but her wolf wanted freedom first and took off into a run.

He soon caught up to them, and they ran together as her wolf explored these woods. Sniffing different trees, noticing certain rocks, taking in details to remember their way back, like a person would remember roads and houses. They playfully tackled each other in openings in the trees and hunted squirrels and rabbits together. Lilian didn't know if she would ever get used to sensing the warm, coppery blood her wolf ate during the kills, but she knew her wolf put up with her crap all the time, so it was a tradeoff.

When her wolf felt sated from eating enough and having enough time to run, she began the slow walk back towards their home. Lilian felt her wolf's tail twitch back and forth. She was teasing Dylan's wolf like a human would sensually walk to a bedroom. It didn't take long to work either. Just as they reached a clearing covered in a bed of leaves, they felt the weight of another wolf on their back and tried to playfully knock him off. Fangs nipped into their shoulder to hold them in place as the other wolf thrust himself into them. As his knot released, her wolf cried out in surprise and pleasure. Lilian herself jumped a bit inside. She never looked up how dogs mated and were not prepared for this. She wasn't sure whether she liked it or if it was too strange. The only thing she did know was that her wolf seemed to love the love bite and knot. *Wait... Can this make us pregnant? Would I have puppies? Oh no. I have to remember to ask Dylan. Will that be an awkward conversation?*

Once Dylan's wolf was spent, the knot released, and he pulled out of her wolf. Now her wolf was sated in every way and definitely pleased with herself as she did a sashay style walk back to their home. Lilian mentally shook her head at her wolf's antics. They soon arrived at the backside of the house. Lilian did as Dylan had instructed her. She thought about her human, fully-clothed self and the feeling she had during the initial shift. Once she opened her eyes, she was relieved to see she was back to herself. *Wait a minute... Not my new bra and underwear!* she thought in dismay as she covered her face with her hand.

"Is something wrong?" Dylan asked as he walked up beside her.

"Well. I shifted back, and I do have clothes on," she stated.

"Okay?"

"I pictured what I looked like, not what I wore underneath..."

He took her by the hips and rubbed up against her. "You mean you have nothing on under this shirt and pants?" he asked, raising an eyebrow.

Lilian could feel his attraction to her at that moment as he stiffened inside his shorts. "Yup. I'd be basically naked if it weren't for this shirt and my pants." She licked her lips, his eyes following her every movement.

"I could help you remedy that," he offered.

She couldn't help but laugh. "Oh, I'm sure you could."

Before she could say anything more, he claimed her mouth. He nipped at the lip where she had just licked it, as if marking her lips as his. The hands holding her hips slowly slid up her stomach beneath her shirt, making trails of warmth leading up to her chest. Before he could go too far, Lilian pressed her hands on his chest and broke the kiss. "Not outside," she said. She wouldn't be naked or having sex with him outside when the other shifters were out roaming around.

Dylan crooked his brow, and Lilian found herself in his arms. She laughed and wrapped her arms around his neck. He carried her all the way into the house and straight to the bedroom, where he did remedy her clothing problem. This time there was no pain, no cramps, nothing that woke her up as they slept afterward. The medicine she was taking was a miracle.

Chapter 13

The day was here. Surgery day. Lilian was a nervous wreck but excited. Excited for answers, possible relief, and to hopefully learn the pain wasn't just in her head as the school nurse had once told her. Dr. Johnson had already been in to talk to her about the plans for surgery and to get her consent to do anything necessary. They talked about the sedation and the aftercare at home. Dr. Johnson also gave Dylan a packet of instructions just in case Lilian forgot.

She was now sitting on the hospital bed in the oh-so-lovely gown. Her stomach grumbled because she couldn't have anything to eat or drink since last night. Lilian wondered how she would feel after surgery. Some people were able to eat normally, while others had to take it easy because of nausea and pain.

The way her stomach was talking, she was hoping for normal.

At 8 o'clock on the dot, Dr. Johnson walked in with an assistant and the anesthesiologist. The latter talked to her about how she would be put to sleep and might wake up groggy and to let him know if she felt anything too strange in case of a reaction. After she nodded in understanding, she said goodbye to Dylan, and they wheeled her away to the operating room.

It was strange to be in a room so white and so cold. She could see the robotics Dr. Johnson would use to make small incisions instead of large ones by hand. *I wonder if using those would be similar to Dylan playing a video game,* she mused, trying to calm her nerves. They had her transfer from the bed to the operating table before she was put to sleep...

When she slowly woke up, she could hear typing on the computer as a nurse recorded her vitals from the blood pressure cuff that helped wake her up with its vice-like grip. She didn't feel much pain since they had given her pain meds through the IV she still had attached to her forearm. She tried moving her legs to make sure they worked and felt an odd feeling. *It must be the catheter they told me about so I wouldn't pee on the table during surgery.* Picturing herself doing something like that made her giggle.

"Oh, good! You're awake," the nurse said. "Do you feel like you will be able to stay awake? If so, we can remove the catheter and try seeing if you can pee normally in a bit."

"I think so," Lilian said. Having never done anything like this before, she didn't know what the nurse was talking about but figured she would just go along with her.

When the catheter was out, she did feel a bit more normal. The nurse brought her some Z-up to drink and a couple packets of saltine crackers. "Let's see how your stomach does and if we can get you to use the bathroom soon. Once we see that you are fully functioning, you can go home and rest."

"Where's Dylan?" she asked.

"He is still out in the waiting area. He couldn't be back here until you were awake and could tell us you were ready for company."

"I see. Well, he can come back whenever he wants," Lilian said to give the nurse permission to let him in. She hoped he would come right away. She wanted his company and him to be with her just in case. In case of what? She didn't know. She just wanted him.

Lilian continued to sip on her drink, having already eaten the crackers. She was sitting up and covered with the sheet-like blanket they had given her when the nurse returned with Dylan in tow.

"How are you feeling?" he asked. His voice was soft and shaking from his own nervousness. Lilian thought he was being cute. He really cared deeply for her, and she wondered if he wore a trail in the waiting room floor from pacing.

"So far, I'm all right," she said. "I have eaten crackers and had some soda but haven't tried moving yet. It'll be a different story when the pain relievers wear off."

The nurse chimed in, "Before you leave, we will give you some more plus a prescription to fill at the pharmacy. If you take them on time, you should feel okay. You just can't overdo it, even if you do feel well enough because it could set things back."

"I understand," Lilian told her. "I'm also pretty sure that Dylan will make sure I have a boring time full of rest at home," she added with a smile in his direction.

"You bet!" he confirmed, giving them all a laugh.

Dr. Johnson took that time to walk into her room. "Are you feeling up to hearing about your surgery? If not, I can call you in a few days."

"No, I'm okay," Lilian said. Even if she wasn't, she wanted to know and not have to wait.

"You were right. There was endometriosis on your uterus, tubes, and ovaries. There was also some on your colon and stomach, which I removed. There was a lot of scarred tissue, though. You didn't have an appendix, so you must have had surgery to remove that when you were fairly young since you didn't remember it. The healing from that started the scarring, and the sticky tissue spread over the years, fusing some of your organs together. Between the scarring and the endo, your ovary and bladder stuck to your uterus, and your gallbladder was also covered. I removed as much of the endo and scarred tissue that I could find, un-fused everything, and removed your gallbladder so it wouldn't cause you future issues. While in there, I decided to flush out your fallopian tubes to ensure there were no clogs and that everything could be functional in case you decide to try for children."

"Wait, I can have children? I thought the endo would have made me infertile."

"It can definitely cause challenges, but usually infertility is also caused by other issues added on top of the endo. One of them I do want to talk to you about." Dr. Johnson paused, deciding how to say it without being too medical. "Remember your bloodwork?"

"Yes. I remember there being a lot of vials."

Dr. Johnson nodded. "Those were all the tests to check your vitamin levels, hormones, and things like cholesterol and blood sugars since you haven't been to a doctor in years. Only a few tests came back a bit odd. One was your severely low vitamin C, so we will get you on a prescription vitamin for that. The test basically says you have inflammation, which came back elevated, but that's normal for endo patients or anyone with chronic pain. Now the last one is your progesterone." The doctor gave Lilian a hard look that said this next part was serious before she continued.

"When you had your tests done, it was around the time when you would have been ovulating. However, your progesterone was severely deficient and should have been much higher. This tells us that you may not be producing an egg every month, and if you did become pregnant, we would have to make sure your progesterone increases. If it doesn't, you would need a supplement because that hormone helps the fetus implant and stay viable. Low progesterone is one of the main causes of miscarriages. Everything should be fine *if* we catch your pregnancy early and give you medicine during the first sixteen weeks." Dr. Johnson put emphasis on the 'if we catch' part and Lilian understood that she had to be vigilant and pay better attention to her body going forward.

"I know you are only just eighteen, so this is all hypothetical right now. I just wanted you to know now to possibly save you future heartache. If you do try and can't seem to get pregnant, just send me an email and I will prescribe you something to help. Sound like a plan?"

Lilian nodded and gave the doctor a smile. She felt relieved to have answers and excited now for a future of possibilities. "Thank you for telling me all of that.

It was a lot of information, but I think I understood it all. Also, thank you for not dismissing me when we first talked. I am in a social media group where many women are dismissed by doctors and have to see several before one will actually listen and try to help. I really appreciate all you have done. It sounds like I was just as much of a hot mess on the inside as I am on the outside," she joked.

"Yeah, you were." Dr. Johnson laughed in agreement. "But you should be great when you recover. If any pain returns, please reach out to me so we can catch any regrowth immediately." She gave Lilian a nod as if to solidify that they both agreed to her request. She shook their hands and then left the room.

"I'm hoping you will remember all that pregnancy information," Dylan said. "I was trying to follow along, but I don't know anything about that stage, except how to get there, of course." He smirked. Lilian and the nurse shared a look and then shook their heads. *Boys.*

"Well, then," her nurse said. "Do you feel like you can try the bathroom? We can't release you until you can move around and use the bathroom on your own."

"I can try," Lilian said. When she tried to swing her legs over to the side of the bed, she felt some pain in her abdomen. Dylan held out his hand, and she used it to help herself sit up on the edge as she gritted her teeth. This pain obviously felt different from her old pain, but it wasn't as bad. *I can handle this,* she told herself.

Dylan stood up and held his hands again in case she needed help standing. She managed to get to her feet before dizziness hit. She gripped onto his arms and waited for the room to stop spinning. The nurse came around the bed and waited patiently for her to get her bearings. When Lilian began to walk, the nurse helped move the IV pole and followed her into the en suite bathroom. Once Lilian sat down, the nurse left the room and closed the door behind her.

Lilian sat there for a few minutes. It felt like she was trying to retrain her brain on how to use the bathroom. But when did it connect? "Oh my freaking GODS, it burns!"

"Is she okay?" she could hear Dylan asking the nurse.

"She's fine," the nurse replied. "I didn't want to warn her that the catheter can make things a bit sensitive because when people hear that, they tense up and then can't go. It usually only burns the first time, and then she'll feel normal the next time."

"If you're sure…"

While Lilian could understand the nurse's reasons, she did wish she had a warning. Now that the initial pain and shock were gone, it didn't burn as much. But *wow*. She hadn't expected that at all. *Talk about unexpected torture.*

When she felt empty, Lilian stood up slowly so she didn't get dizzy again. The toilet flushed, and she walked the IV pole over to the sink to wash her hands. She couldn't help but look in the mirror at her mass of tangled hair. Thankfully, her hairbrush was in the bag she'd brought with her. Lilian opened the bathroom door and walked back to the bed to prove she could get around. Her abdomen felt tight and bruised, but she wasn't going to show it. *I suffered for six years. This is nothing,* she thought to herself to help her focus.

The nurse did notice her efforts. "If you feel up to it, I can go and get your discharge paperwork, and we can remove the IV. After that, you can get dressed and head home to bed."

"I think I'm ready for that," Lilian said. The nurse left to get the papers, leaving her alone with Dylan. She sat down on the edge of the bed like before. "Can you get my bag from over in the corner? I can at least start getting my lower half dressed and maybe start untangling my hair if it takes her a while."

"I will get it, but I'll help you, so you aren't trying to bend too much," he said.

By the time the nurse returned, Dylan already had her shoes on her, and he had brushed her hair nest out. "I'm not sure which of you is more excited to go home," the nurse joked.

"I think we both are." Lilian giggled. A spark of pain hit her stomach. "Ouch, maybe laughing isn't a good thing right now."

"Laughing, sneezing, and coughing will be a bit painful for the next week," said the nurse. "I did bring you a couple pain pills to take with your soda before you head out. It should help you feel well enough to ride in the wheelchair to the pharmacy and then the truck."

"Thank you," Lilian told her gratefully. She grabbed the tiny medicine cup and swallowed the pills before finishing her drink. Then she held out her arm for the nurse to unchain her from the IV pole.

Soon she was freed, and they were heading home, with her medicine in her lap for safe keeping.

Chapter 14

Lilian missed Thanksgiving at Dylan's parents' house since she was still recovering then, but she was feeling great by Christmas! She had even shifted during the last full moon. Sure, those first two weeks were rough, especially when her body decided she needed to have sneezing fits.

She was also off the norethindrone now that she had surgery and wanted to see how she would do without it. The bad part about not taking it was getting her period. She had been warned by the Nook group how the first couple would be the worst, and they were not kidding. When it started, she thought she was dying before she realized it was just her cycle kick starting back up with a bang.

Now that those five long days were over, she was able to enjoy her body and how great it felt. In fact,

Dylan was also enjoying how great her body felt more often than before. No longer did she feel broken, but she was still questioned whether or not she was. She continued to think that, as a Luna, she needed to be able to have children. In fact, pack members constantly asked Dylan and his parents when they might be trying for a family. Dylan would just tell them that they were taking time to enjoy themselves first.

His parents still wouldn't give up, though. They went to their house for Christmas dinner and to exchange presents. The Alpha gave his sons watches because, he joked, "Maybe they will help you be on time for meetings." The Luna gave them clothes and told Lilian it was because her boys never thought to get themselves any until there were holes in every single thing. Having seen a couple of those holes, Lilian couldn't help but agree with her.

Lilian had gone shopping with Dylan to get his parents and brother gifts, yet she was surprised that they had also gotten her presents. This was the first Christmas she had ever celebrated. Her dad had never remembered the holidays when he was alive, and Lilian didn't celebrate when he was gone either. Seeing what they thought she liked or could use was nice. Well, except for a couple of unisex baby onesies that talked about "what happens at grandma's stays at grandma's."

"Really, mom?" Dylan asked.

Luna Marianne shrugged and said, "Someday, they will get used." Lilian couldn't help but laugh it off and repeat, "Someday."

It was a nice feeling having a family celebration. She knew there would be many more to come. More to get used to. After dinner and presents, they all sat in the living room to enjoy a Christmas movie before going home to bed. Dylan and Lilian did go home, and they went to bed... to have their own celebration.

Only one month later, Lilian's wolf refused to let her shift. Mentioning it to Dylan, he told her, "There's only a couple of reasons why she wouldn't shift. One is if you were too hurt to concentrate on shifting. The other is if... you're pregnant?" he ended it with a question.

"Am I?" she asked. She watched Dylan rush out the door and climb into his truck. He took off down the road, leaving Lilian totally confused. He returned less than thirty minutes later with a bag from the center.

He gave her the bag and told her to take it to the bathroom.

When Lilian got there, she saw all the different brands and types of pregnancy tests, picked the one that looked easiest to read, and used it. Sitting it on the counter, she opened the door to a waiting Dylan, and they stood together in silence while counting the seconds that passed.

When it was time, they looked at it together. It was clear. "Pregnant" was spelled out in bold, black digital letters.

"Umm," said Dylan. "We better call Dr. Johnson and tell her we had a Christmas miracle."

Just eight months later, after constant nausea and thirty pounds of added weight, they were able to meet Adelynne as she came into the world... Lilian was able to feel whole for the first time in her life.

Author Notes

T hank you for reading my story. The feelings and information presented throughout are based on my own battle with endometriosis. It isn't a one-size-fits-all type of disease, but it is real and not just "in our heads".

I released this novella on October 4th in recognition of, not only, Mental Health Awareness week but also World Day of Bullying Prevention, as well as Bullying Prevention month.

Mentioned in this story is a social media group called Nancy's Nook. The Nook is an actual group that can be found on Facebook. Its full name is Nancy's Nook Endometriosis Education. There is also a website, NancysNookEndo.com, where even more resources are located.

If you, or a loved one, suspect they may have en-dometriosis, please research to be a better advocate for yourself and others. There is still a ton of myths and misinformation surrounding endo out there, includ-ing beliefs still held by some medical professionals. The more you know, the better you can find the right help.

About the Author

L ore Nicole lives on a family dairy farm with her husband and three children in Southwestern Wisconsin. She likes to include pieces of herself in every story, whether it be a situation she has faced (endometriosis) or a character trait (neurospicy). Her goal is to help spread awareness of tough subjects, hoping the stories may help even just one person find answers, or to even feel less alone.

To stay up-to-date on her current and future stories, visit AuthorsoftheQuill.com. While there, you will see her other pen names, and can also sign up for her monthly newsletter. If you enjoy reading serial fiction, look at more stories here: AuthorsoftheQuill.com/V ellas